Missing Emily: Croatian Life Letters

Jodie Toohey

**Wordsy Woman
Press**

ISBN: 0692414274
ISBN-13: 978-0692414279 (Wordsy Woman Press)

FOR KATIE LEA
AND YOU

ACKNOWLEDGMENTS

Many special thanks to my good friend, Biljana. This book would not have been possible without you. Your experiences gave me the idea for this book and your extensive help brought it to fruition. Thank you so much for opening up to me over our several conversations. Thank you, also, for your encouragement, guidance, and fun lunches. I look forward to a lasting friendship.

Thanks to my critique partner, Connie Heckert. Your guidance, edits, suggestions, and title definitely made this book much better.

To Midwest Writing Center: Thank you for all of the connections, information, instruction, encouragement, and support as I've transitioned to full-time writer.

Finally, thanks to my husband, kids, mom, family, and friends who may not always understand me, but, nevertheless, freely give their encouragement and support.

Jodie Toohey

A NOTE ABOUT CROATIAN WORD PRONUNCIATION

Most of the Croatian words used in this book sound like they are spelled, except for several key differences:

The letter "Č" or "Ć" makes the "CH" sound like in the word, "church." "DJ" or "dj" takes the hard "G" sound like in "giant."

"J" or "j" makes the "Y" sound as in "yellow."

The combination of "lj" makes the sound, "lli", like in "trillion."

The letter "Š" or "š" makes the "SH" sound like in "shape."

The letter "Ž" or "ž" makes the English "J" sound like in "Jump."

The letter "e" appearing at the end of a name makes the sound, "EH."

CHAPTER ONE

Just a box of letters; a box of life-saving letters. I crossed my legs, lifted the lid, and let the dust bunnies fall to the floor. I hadn't looked at that box in over a year. They were all there: the first short, impersonal letter all the way through to the last birthday card. All of them started the same way: the date with the day of the month first, and then, "Dear Ami." I put the box in my pile of things to take to college. I tried to continue cleaning my room, an offering of a law school study office for my mom. My mind kept taking me back. I remembered the first of the cataclysmic events causing the sharp turn eventually leading to the life and death decision that brought me here.

The date is etched in my memory: March 7, 1990. Mom had planned to start law school that year. She and my dad had an agreement; she would support him while he became a doctor and got established, and then she could attend law school. Mom always wanted to be a lawyer. She convinced Dad to let her name all of her children after Latin court terms. She planned, saved, and read everything she could related to the law to stay motivated. Always full of unwelcome surprises, Dad changed these plans. He had been working as a surgical fellow for only a few months when Mom received her acceptance letter to law school in the mail.

When I came down for dinner that night, there were only three plates on the table.

"Eating late with Dad again?" I asked.

"Yes, and I want you kids to go to bed early," she said.

"What? How early? I'm in …"

"You don't have to go to sleep; just stay in your rooms. I'm surprising Daddy with a candlelit fettuccine Alfredo dinner."

"His favorite?"

"Yes. I'm going to share my good news."

"Good news?"

"I got my letter today. I'm going to law school."

"Congratulations!" I hugged her.

Later, I lay in bed reading a book with the door open just enough to hear what was going on downstairs. I listened for the bursts of laughter as my dad congratulated Mom on her achievement, well-deserved after all she'd given up for him. When, for several minutes all I heard was silence, I snuck out and crouched behind the wall in the hallway at the top of the stairs.

Dad said, "We've grown apart. You have nothing to talk about but the kids and the house. We're not on the same level intellectually anymore. Being a father isn't 'me.' I'm moving in with Nikki."

Nikki was his surgical nurse who had just passed her boards.

He said, "Nikki makes me feel young again and I don't

have to wait to travel because Nikki has already started her career. I don't want to wait for three years for you to finish law school."

They were silent.

My dad continued, his voice a high-pitched whistle, "I'll still do what I can to help you through law school. I'll take the kids every other weekend and a couple of weeks in the summer. I'll even take them to dinner one evening a week so you can study."

Finally, Mom spoke, "So you're saying being a husband and full- time father is not *convenient* anymore so you're *quitting*?"

"Yeah, I guess so." Dad choked. "I know, it sounds terrible."

I sat immobilized, staring at the wall in front of me. The swirls in the textured paint began to meld together. I couldn't move even as I heard Dad's footsteps thud on the carpet-padded stairs.

"Amicus." I heard my name as if my dad was on the other side of the play tunnel we played in at the park on Sundays when I was little. "Ami, are you okay?"

I turned slowly toward the voice. He jumped, startled, like he hadn't realized I was there.

He gasped. "You look just like your mother."

I wasn't sure what he meant. Mom's hair was dark brown and fell halfway down her back in soft waves while mine was a dirty, ashy blond that plunged like tiny long toothpicks to my shoulders. She was curvy while I forgot to "develop." Even though I was fourteen at the time, the sides of my torso still made basically straight lines to my feet. Our eyes were blue so I thought maybe that was what he meant.

Millions of questions bounced around my head, but I

could not pull any two words together. I think I may have squeaked a couple of times before Dad briefly rested his hand on the top of my head. He stepped over my legs on his way to their bedroom down the hall. A few minutes later, he came out with the duffle bag he used to take when he was on all-night call at the hospital as a resident, again stepped over me, and went down the stairs. I heard the careful soft click of the front door closing. The house remained still, like it was holding its breath, until the sunlight coming in my parents' bedroom window stretched into the hallway and Prio woke up, demanding breakfast.

At that moment, everything changed, but at the same time, nothing changed. Life seemed to become more mechanical. I didn't really notice Dad not living with us anymore; he had been gone so much during medical school, his residency, and fellowship, he was hardly there anyway. My mom still took care of our house and us. She took us to school, fixed our lunches, read Prio picture books before bed, and helped Forti plan the perfect item to take to show and tell. She still asked me how my day was when I got home from school, but she seemed to stop caring about the answers. I was the oldest, so I guess they thought I understood the nuances and struggles inherent in a marriage and in its ending. I suppose it was partly my fault. Forti and Prio constantly demanded Mom's time and I saw how this frustrated her.

One night, I decided I would talk to Mom about still going to law school. I loaded the dishwasher after dinner. Mom sat at the kitchen table, leaning on her elbows. She looked like she was about to fall asleep. Forti and Prio giggled as they wrestled in the living room.

"I'll get Forti and Prio to bed if you want," I said.

"What?" Her head fell toward the table and then she

snapped up. "Oh, no, that's okay. Prio needs a bath."

"I can give Prio his bath."

She stood up. "Actually, that would be great." She gave me a slight wave as she shuffled away.

I finally got Prio bathed and tucked in. I made sure Forti was in bed and approached Mom's bedroom. She was face-down on her bed in her clothes, snoring. I tried again the next night, only to find her lying on her bed crying into her pillow. After that, I decided the best way to help was to be easy, so I retreated to the shadows, doing everything I could to avoid drawing attention.

Our early 1980s two-story house became devoid of hope, no longer working or planning for the day it would become something great. Over the summer, the weeds quickly suffocated the brilliant colors of impatiens, petunias, and whatever newest blooming perennial Mom planted last fall in the flower beds in front of our windows in her annual, hopeless attempt to sustain life in something other than impatiens and petunias. Even during the severe dry summer of 1988, she stopped everything to go out at dusk to water her flowers, the only time it was allowed by the city. That summer, though not as dry as '88, did not provide enough water to sustain the flowers, so they withered and died. The only bright spot became Saturday nights.

I anxiously waited for every Saturday. That's when I got to babysit my cousin, Emily, while Aunt Shari and Uncle Matt went out for dinner. I started to babysit Emily when she was a baby. Before Dad left, just Mom and I would go to Aunt Shari's house on Sunday afternoons when he wasn't working so Aunt Shari could have some "adult female conversation" and I could look after and play with baby Emily. Mom convinced Dad that Aunt Shari needed us without the distraction of Forti and Prio. Most of the time, Uncle Matt went to our house to watch sports with Dad. Forti and Prio never complained and seemed happy when we returned, so we never asked if they had actually spent time with my dad or if they just played in their rooms. I asked my mom once what they did when Uncle Matt came over, and she said as long as the house was in one piece and nothing was broken, she didn't care. As long as it didn't take me away from time with Emily, I didn't care either. After Dad moved out, on Sunday afternoons I was with him at his house or he was spending "quality time" with Nikki so he couldn't keep Forti and Prio.

All four of us tried to visit Aunt Shari once. Mom and Aunt Shari drank coffee at the dining room table. I held Emily and tried to keep Forti and Prio occupied with a video. Every time Aunt Shari opened her mouth, either Forti or Prio summoned my mom.

"I want to hold Emmy," Prio said.

"Sit on the couch and I will put her in your arms." I showed him how to hold his arms like a cradle and laid Emily in them. She squirmed.

"Hold still," he whispered.

"You're not doing it right," Forti said. "Look at her. She doesn't like it. It's my turn." Forti pulled Emily's bare foot toward her.

"Forti, stop it. You're hurting her!" Emily started to scream. Big tears flowed down her cheeks and it broke my heart.

I picked her up and hugged her to my chest. "Now look what you did."

"What is going on here?" Mom, with Aunt Shari close behind, walked in from the dining room. Forti and Prio pointed at and talked over each other.

Aunt Shari kneeled down in front of Forti and Prio on the couch. "Emily is getting bigger and she doesn't like to be held as much anymore."

"Ami gets to hold her," Forti said.

"Ami and Emily have a special bond, I guess," Aunt Shari said.

"I'm sorry, Shari. Maybe we will have to plan our visits when Don can take care of the little ones," Mom said.

"But, Mom." A lump started to form in my throat. "When will I get to see her?" I kissed Emily's forehead. "I'll miss her too much."

"I have an idea," Aunt Shari said. "Matt and I need to spend more time together. And since Emily is over six months old, I'll feel more comfortable leaving her with a babysitter. Maybe we can plan a regular date night and Ami can babysit."

So I took a babysitting class and started to babysit Emily every Saturday night.

Each week, Saturday night could not come fast enough. After Dad left, I didn't feel like hanging out with Krissa or my other friends anymore. After a while, they stopped calling me, and then they stopped inviting me to their birthday parties. But I didn't care because I would rather spend time in my bed listening to music and Saturday nights with Emily. The only person I really would've wanted to hear from was Larry Benson and I knew there was no way that would happen.

When Emily was a newborn, I held her for hours, watching her sleep and feeding her when she woke up. When she got a little older, I talked to her to make her smile and laugh. When she could sit up, I taught her to play patty cake, and when she started to crawl, I crawled right behind her. I knew she loved me; she was the only one whose love I never questioned. When I arrived to start babysitting after she was walking, she would run over the hardwood floors, dragging her pink baby blanket behind, her face lit up with a smile, brown hair a wild mess, squealing. I would crouch down, open my arms as wide as I could, and as soon as she got close enough, clamp them tight around her little body, lift her, and twirl in circles. It was the music and Emily that kept me sane.

CHAPTER TWO

Tears fell into the dust, creating mud puddles under the bed. I leaned back against the mattress and pulled the box of Nada's letters back into my lap. I remembered that date as well: February 13, 1991.

It was the day before Valentine's Day, and rather than anticipating a fabulous romantic date, I was in ninth grade English class. Most of my classmates would say they were *stuck* in ninth grade English class, but if I couldn't be with Emily, I would rather be at school. At school, I could temporarily forget the darkness at home; I could lose myself in studying and getting good grades.

I anticipated another assignment at which I could excel when my teacher waved a stack of jaggedly cut copy-machine copied paper in the air. "I will be giving each of you a piece of paper with a name and address."

The boys in the class snickered. I looked up. Two large puddles of sweat flanked each of Mrs. Abernathy's armpits.

Camanche High's thermostat was governed randomly,

neither by the calendar nor the temperature. It was cold and windy as it often was in mid-February, but it was easily 80° in the windowless classroom.

As Mrs. Abernathy handed out the identities of our new pen pals, I stared at the blank page. I wrote, "Dear," left a few spaces, indented, and rested the tip of my pen on the paper. I started to move it to create a letter, but stopped. Finally, Mrs. Abernathy placed a piece of paper face-down on the corner of the desk. I snatched it up and flipped it over.

"Who did you get?" Krissa tapped my back with the eraser of her pencil from her desk right behind mine. "What's your country?"

Krissa and I had hardly spoken to each other in weeks. I twisted in the chair. "It says Crow at ti ya, Yugoslavia."

"Crow-at-ti-ya? Where's that?"

I muttered, "I don't know." Geography was never a good subject for me. I held the paper in the air to get my teacher's attention.

"Yes, Amicus, do you have a question?"

"Where is Crow-at-ti-ya?"

"Crow-eh-ti-who?"

I spread the paper taut between both hands and pointed the printed side toward Mrs. Abernathy. She hunched over and walked toward me, her hands clasped behind her back. Her long, black hair hung down in twisted strings from behind her ears and dangled toward the floor. She pushed the sweat from her forehead back into her hairline and squinted. "That's not Crow-at-ti-ya, it's pronounced Crow-eh-shuh."

"Croatia," I whispered.

Mrs. Abernathy grabbed a rubber band from under Andy Marlin's desk across the aisle from me and twisted it around her hair. She missed a few pieces and looked like she'd just been captured after running away from the police. The boys snickered again.

"Does anyone else have any questions?"

"Where's Paraguay?" Marcus Reynolds blurted, his hands clenching under his desk. He winked at me. I couldn't decide if he was making fun of me or trying to make me feel better.

"I'll tell you what." Mrs. Abernathy plopped down in her wooden rolling desk chair. She pushed her shirt sleeves into her armpits. She guzzled half of the bottle of water sitting on the corner of her desk and held its sweaty plastic to her neck. She pulled her beach ball-sized cardboard globe from the other corner of her desk, blew the dust from the North Pole, and sat it in front of her. "Anyone who wants to see where their pen pal's country is located, or has any other questions, raise your hand."

At least half the hands in the class shot up in the air. Apparently, I was not the only one who had trouble with geography.

"Sit down." Mrs. Abernathy sighed. "Put your hands down. Let's try this again. Now listen very carefully." She sucked in deep. "Do not move until I say, 'go.' If you want me to show you where your pen pal's country is on the globe, raise one hand in the air."

Aaron Barrington was the class clown. His hand sprouted straight up.

Mrs. Abernathy said, "Mr. Barrington. I did not say 'go.'"

A few of the girls' giggles puffed out through their hands clasped over their mouths and Aaron slunk back into his seat, pretending remorse, "Sorry, Mrs. Abernathy."

"As I was saying, raise one hand in the air and hold it stiff like a flag pole." Mrs. Abernathy used to teach kindergarten. "I will call your name to come to my desk. While you wait for me to call your name, begin writing your letters." Mrs. Abernathy took another big drag from her water bottle. "Okay." She hesitated. "Go."

I raised my right hand but I write with that hand. I switched arms. I wrote "Dear Nada," but the carbon paper I used so I could have a copy of my letter danced under the force of the shifting pen. It was so sloppy I had to start over. I pinned the paper beneath my left elbow, my hand still as high in the air as I could get it, and finally created two legible words.

"Amicus, do you have a question?"

I blew eraser bits from the paper and stuck my hand back into pole formation. "Yes." I walked behind Mrs. Abernathy's desk.

She turned the globe. I recognized North America.

"Where are we?" she said.

I looked at the small print.

"Well, *about* where are we?" Her faced was flushed. I looked up and did not see any more hands in the air. I quickly touched the tip of my right index finger to the middle of the United States on the globe.

Mrs. Abernathy spun the globe silently and pointed to a country nearly on the opposite side of the sphere. I read, "Yugoslavia."

"Then here is Croatia, a republic within Yugoslavia." She used the tip of her red pen to invisibly outline an area that looked like an alligator's head with another republic in its mouth. The small islands along its southern coast looked like dripping saliva.

"Where is this?" I pointed to the word on my paper. I didn't want to embarrass myself again.

Mrs. Abernathy held a magnifying glass to the globe and

sat her pen on a tiny dot between the alligator's lower jaw and dripping saliva, the spot on the its neck where you'd scratch it if it were a cat or a dog. "The 'j' is pronounced like a 'y.' It's pronounced, Rijeka."

I returned to my desk and wrote:

*   *   *   *   *

February 13, 1991

Dear Nada,

How are you? I guess I am fine. I am writing this letter to you because it is today's English class assignment. But I don't mind. I like to write letters.

I am fifteen years old. I am in the ninth grade at Camanche High School in Camanche, Iowa, in the United States of America. I live with my mom, sister, and brother in a two-story house. My mom's name is Sue.

My name is Amicus but all of my friends call me Ami. You can call me Ami if you want to. My parents named all of their kids after Latin legal terms. Clearly, Amicus is the best one; it means "friend of the court." Afortiori, which means "with stronger reason," is my sister's name. We call her Forti. She is eight years old. Apriori, which means "from cause to effect," is my baby brother (well, he is not really a baby anymore because he is four but I still call him that). His nickname is Prio.

What do you do for fun? I love to spend time with my little

cousin, Emily. She is 16 months old and she is the only thing that can make me smile. I used to like to ride bikes or go for walks on next to the Mississippi River, shop at the mall, and roller skate with friends but not so much anymore. When I'm not with Emily, I love listening to music; it takes me away.

The bell is going to ring in five minutes so I have to go. Please write me back.

Your New Pen Pal,
Amicus Sinkey

*   *   *   *   *

I turned my letter into Mrs. Abernathy. After class, I passed Larry Benson's locker. He leaned against the metal talking to Heather Birch. I fought the urge to reach around him to feel whether the cool metal of his locker was as warmed by Larry's presence as I was. A passing elbow collided with mine, sending my books flying to the floor in slow motion. I dropped to pick them up and avoided glancing in Larry's and Heather's direction as I nearly sprinted to my locker, my face burning. *Did he see it? Or worse, did he not see me at all?*

CHAPTER THREE

I didn't think again about the letter until I arrived home from school the first day of March to find a thin envelope addressed to me with a border around the outside like a red, white, and blue candy cane and several cancelled stamps on our kitchen counter. I examined it. The only mail I ever received was a magazine for teens and the occasional erroneously addressed junk mail. Both addresses were printed neatly, all the letters capitalized and uniformly sized but for the "j" in Rijeka, which finally triggered my memory. I dropped my backpack to the floor and carefully released the envelope flap. I pulled out a neatly folded, blue lined paper just like I used every day and read.

* * * * *

23 February 1991

Dear Ami,

I was excited to receive your letter. My friend, Sanja, and I talk about living in America one day. I hope you are able to understand my English. Many people here speak English. It is same in other cities on the edge of the Adriatic Sea where I live. I am still learning to write in English in school. Luckily I was not put into German like my sister, Maja, or we would not be able to write to each other.

Maja is eleven years old. She is in grade five. I am thirteen years old. I am in grade seven. I have no brothers. It is just Maja; Mama, Rada; Tata, Boško; and me. Everyone in my family has dark brown hair and eyes.

Tata is a postman. Mama works as a seamstress in a business suit factory. Perhaps you did not have the time to explain to me your parents' work. I hope if you have more time when you write your next letter to me, you will tell me?

As I mentioned, like you do, I live by water. I live next to Adriatic Sea. It is so beautiful and so blue. Is your Mississippi River like that? It is still cold and wintery here now so I do homework and play with Maja at home when not practicing Tae Kwon Do. I cannot wait for summer. Then I can go swimming in the sea, play outside with friends, and ride bicycles.

I await your reply.

Your new friend,
Nada Popović

∗   ∗   ∗   ∗   ∗

I rushed to reply to Nada's letter. I was halfway up the stairs when my mom yelled, "Ami, your backpack!" I rolled my eyes and skipped down.

I muttered, "Sorry," to Mom as I snatched my backpack from the floor by her feet.

When I arrived to my bedroom, I flung the backpack onto my bed and carefully closed my door. I felt bad for irritating Mom. It filled my heart with pride on the occasions she would smile at me while I was eating my cereal and say, "Ami, you are so quiet; I hardly know you're here." But I had a letter to write.

I sat down at the wood desk Mom found at a garage sale and gave to me after the first day of kindergarten. She told me I needed to start my education off on the right foot and she spent a week rearranging my small bedroom to fit the desk against the pink and purple striped walls. I dug my best stationary and carbon paper out from the bottom desk drawer, careful not to move the desk too much and dislodge the folded-up pieces of cardboard steadying it on the carpet. I got a purple ink pen and wrote the date at the top of the page, March 1, 1991. I shifted the paper higher on my desk, rested the pen's tip on the paper, and stared at the wall.

I adored the purple and pink stripes when I was five but despised them by the time I was ten. Mom said she spent so much time painting the neat stripes that I had to live with them until I went to college. I even offered to paint them, but she said she didn't think I was mature enough to paint carefully and not ruin my carpeting. So I did what I could to cover the walls using poster putty to pin up posters of the *Beverly Hills 90210* stars, Tom Cruise, the guys from *Saved By The Bell*, and, of course, all of the NKOTB from *Tiger Beat* and *Bop*. I reread Nada's letter to me and decided to first answer her questions. I wrote:

*   *   *   *   *

March 1, 1991

Dear Nada,

My dad's name is Donald Sinkey and he is a doctor; a surgeon to be more specific. My mom's name is Sue Sinkey. For now, she just takes care of us and our house, but she is going to be a great lawyer one day. She had to put her plans on hold when my dad decided he'd rather live with his surgical nurse.

The Adriatic Sea sounds nothing like the Mississippi River, which is brown and muddy. Many people say it is beautiful but I don't see it. There are some bluffs at places along the river high above the water which I think are pretty, but that is not the river. There is one place on the river I like to visit. It is completely full of water lilies; they rise up out of the muddy water like a miracle. Do you have water lilies in your country? If you don't, I will tell you about them. If you do, please ignore the following few sentences. The leaves of the water lilies poke out of the water curled into a tight stick. When they get to the right height, they relax, the leaves uncurl, they sink back to the river, and float on the top like hearts. In July, the water lilies produce sweet smelling blossoms which, if you stand at the right spot, will overtake the smell of dead fish from the river. By the way, when I say "the river," I am referring to the Mississippi River. Everyone here calls it "the river," I guess because it is so big and so much a part of this area. Even though we do have other rivers around here we call them by name and include "river" in their names. We are humoring them because, in comparison to "the river," they are really just streams. Do you call your Adriatic "the sea" or do you use its full name, "Adriatic Sea"?

Do you like music? What kind of music do the teenagers listen to in your country? I LOVE music. I have a small stereo on my dresser in my bedroom. It has a dual cassette deck so I don't have to turn the tapes over so often. Whenever I get any birthday money, I try to buy a new tape or I buy blank tapes and record songs from the radio. I like all different kinds of music. Some of the groups/singers I like are NKOTB, Mariah Carey, Amy Grant, Garth Brooks, and Reba McEntire. My grandma pays me five dollars every once in a while to clean up her house so I have finally saved up enough money to buy Reba McEntire's last album, "Rumor Has It." I have some of the songs I taped off the radio but I like all of the songs so I want the whole tape. Mom said we can go to Target (a store) this weekend to get it. I will tell you if it is good.

Do you have a boyfriend? I wish I did, but I don't.

*   *   *   *   *

"Ami! Dinner!" I jumped in the chair, leaving a trail of ink across my paper. I didn't have time to white it out.

"Coming!" I finished my letter.

*   *   *   *   *

I'm in love with Larry Benson. I will write you more about him later. My mom is calling me for dinner. Write me back when you can. What is it like to live in Croatia and

23

Yugoslavia?

Your friend,
Ami

P.S. SSS (sorry so sloppy)

*   *   *   *   *

I folded the paper, pushed it into its lime green envelope, and scribbled Nada's address on it. My mom, Forti, and Prio were already eating when I reached the kitchen.

"Ami, your food is getting cold," my mom said.

"One sec." I grabbed a return address label and a stamp; I licked them both, stuck them onto the envelope, and then slipped the envelope into the little plastic basket on the counter where we stored outgoing mail. When I slid into my chair at the table, I was thrilled to find the plate covered in meat loaf, mashed potatoes, and brown gravy. I was not so excited to see the pile of carrot cubes there, but I slathered them with butter and salt. I ate them fast before the taste settled on my tongue. That gave me another idea for letters to Nada. I focused on remembering to write a note reminding myself to write to Nada about my favorite foods. Forti and Prio monopolized Mom's attention, as usual, so staying intent on the task was not difficult.

After Forti and I put the clean dishes from the dishwasher away and loaded the dirty dishes into it, I raced back up to my room as fast as I could. I pushed the play button on the right tape deck and "Little Girl" groaned back into motion. Rather than just make a note to talk about food in my next letter to Nada, I decided to get a head start on the actual letter so I

24

could write her back faster after I received her next letter. I never sent it because before I received Nada's next letter, everything fell apart.

Jodie Toohey

CHAPTER FOUR

It was unusually warm and humid at 4:00 p.m. on March 25, 1991. As usual, I retreated to my bedroom after school. I heard the telephone ring in Mom's bedroom through the wall. I assumed it was Grandma's daily call to make sure we all made it home safely. But then I heard urgent footsteps and filled with panic. Forti knocked but didn't wait for an invitation before she swung the door open and said, panting, "Something bad happened. You have to finish cooking dinner."

I jumped from my bed and pushed the mini stereo's power button. The song droned out in low, distorted voices. I hurried to the kitchen. Mom shook as she attempted to tie her shoes.

She said, "Emily was hit by a car. I have to go to the hospital. Finish cooking supper."

"What?" I stammered.

"That was Uncle Matt. He just said she was hit by a car by the park and it was bad."

I watched the door close behind my mom's back. Tears fell into the pan cooking Tuna Helper Au Gratin dinner as I stirred aimlessly. A voice in my head growled, *she's dead*, but I commanded it away and consoled myself. I thought, *She could still be okay. You don't know what happened. Maybe the car just bumped Emily.* I argued with myself, asserting maybe Emily was just in a coma or broke her leg, but negatively retorted, she is so small and cars so big that she could not be anything *but* dead.

I finished cooking dinner and served it with buttered white bread to Forti and Prio. I tried to eat but had only choked down three small tear-laden bites before I was startled by the shrill phone ring. I dreaded answering but picked up the receiver, brought it to my ear in slow motion, and whispered, "Hello."

"She's gone." I thought I had heard Mom wrong, but before I could ask, she said, "She didn't make it."

I yelled, "No," and cried with her through the telephone line. I relayed the message to Forti's and Prio's blank faces. I placed the telephone receiver back on the wall. With a knife twisting in my chest and my stomach constricting, I ran upstairs to the bathroom and vomited into the toilet. I crumbled to the bathroom floor, clutched my stomach, and cried. The trap door had slid from under my feet and I flailed.

Within a few hours, I knew the whole story. Aunt Shari had taken Emily for a walk in her stroller to the park in her neighborhood. When they left to walk back home, Aunt Shari buckled Emily into her stroller. When they reached the intersection a block away from the park, Aunt Shari pushed the street light button and waited for the walk signal. The moment she stepped out into the intersection, an unlicensed sixteen-year-old girl riding with her friends swerved around the cars stopped at the red light and struck Emily's stroller. Aunt Shari tried to hang on to it as it was snatched from her hand and drug under the car. All she could do was watch as Emily's head bounced on the pavement and the car tire traversed her tiny back, causing the massive head injuries which had stolen her life by the time the car stopped several yards away.

The next morning, my family gathered at Grandma and Grandpa's house. Most of the day I sat staring, unable to think of anything but Emily, and screaming to myself, *Why Emily? I loved her with my life!* The funeral director arrived early; he sat at the kitchen table with Grandma, Aunt Shari, and Uncle Matt. I stood on the other side of the kitchen peninsula next to Mom who stood next to Grandpa. Immediately after the arrangements were set and the door closed behind the funeral director, Grandpa broke. The house fell silent and we listened to his agony. My stomach sickened and my throat closed.

He repeated, "Why Emily? Why not me? I am an old man. She was a baby. It should have been me." I looked at Mom; heavy tears rolled down her foundation-smeared cheeks, dropped from her jaw, and pooled on the gold-flecked kitchen countertop. We stood, crying silently, while we waited for my grandpa to resign himself to the fact we could not answer his questions and he could not take Emily's place.

I replayed Emily's entire life in my imagination, wanting to preserve every second in memory. The last time I saw Emily alive was the previous Saturday night. I gave Emily her bath, dried her off with a fluffy towel, and then Emily grabbed the pajamas Aunt Shari had laid out on her bed. She shoved them in front of my face and said, "On!"

I kissed Emily good night and tucked her into bed but she

wouldn't stay. She had just started sleeping in her big-girl bed and enjoyed sneaking out to spy on me from around the corner of the living room wall. I marched her back to bed a few times; the last time I told her sternly, "Emily, it is time to go to sleep. Stay here." She got up once more but I decided to try a different tactic and just ignored her. I peeked in on her a little while later and found her lying perpendicular on her bed. If I had known, I would have kept Emily up and preserved every second of that night.

At the funeral visitation, when the curtains hiding Emily's casket were drawn open, I locked my knees and studied the grape juice colored carpeted floor. Emily lay in the casket in the clothes I picked out with Aunt Shari and my grandma: a pink lavender jumpsuit dotted with tiny white flowers, a white blouse, and saddle shoes. For the first time, Emily's hair was tame. It lay flat, lifeless, and brownish red, still tinted from her blood despite the funeral home's efforts to clean it. She was still. The scrapes on her face were visible through the thick stage-like funeral home makeup. Her skin was cold and rubbery.

After Emily's funeral, I returned to a house covered with a dark cloud filled even more with despair and grief. I was left with a gaping wound that could never heal.

CHAPTER FIVE

Life could not possibly continue and I didn't want it to, but to my amazement and dismay, the sun woke me the following morning. I received another letter from Nada two days after Emily died, but it took me two weeks to open and read it.

*   *   *   *   *

11 March 1991

Dear Ami,

It is so funny. We do call the "Adriatic Sea" just "the sea." But there are really no other seas around to confuse us.

What is school like in America? I guess I like school but it is a lot of work, except for English class. It is my favorite. That is why I signed up for this pen pal project. I love to read and try to write in English. I most specially like to write stories so I like my letters to be like stories.

Mama insists Maja and I go to high school and college. We study all the time so our grades will be high enough to get into high school. I would rather be a hairdresser. Then I wouldn't need good grades but Mama tells me I will not be a hairdresser. She wants me to be a lawyer. My parents work very hard. They did not have any money to go to school when they were kids so they want us to have everything they didn't. I will tell you about my school, then you tell me how your school is same or different.

I started school when I was six years old in first grade. Mama took me to school the first day and ever since then, I walk to school. It is a long walk but it is peaceful. I just went to school in mornings until the grade five. Then my schedule began to alternate each week. One week I will go to school from 8 o'clock in the morning until 2 or 3 in the afternoon. The next week, I go to school from 1 o'clock in the afternoon until 6 or 7 in the evening. The week after that I go back to mornings, then afternoons, then mornings, then afternoons. This continues all through the school year. Our last day of school is usually in middle of June around my birthday on 17 June. We get a month off from school around Christmas time.

When is your birthday? I will be fourteen this year. I hope my parents will let me have a party. It will be so much fun to hang out with friends and dance. We will eat little sandwiches and drink punch. I will also invite my boyfriend, Mate. Mate is so cool and is really nice to me. He takes me for rides on his motorcycle. Tell me about this Larry Benson. Why do you like him? Maybe you can send me a picture. Is he cute? I have a picture of Mate on his motorcycle but it is my only picture so I don't want to send it. I will ask Mate if he has another copy I can send to you.

I am sorry I must end this letter now. I have to finish studying before it is time to go to bed.

Please write back soon!

Your friend,
Nada

*　　*　　*　　*　　*

By then it seemed trivial and irrelevant to continue the letter I started before about food so I started over, but I couldn't finish.

As I read that first letter from Nada after Emily's death, the knot in my throat so familiar then but which I hadn't really remembered was there, took me back. Emily's funeral was on Thursday, March 28th, and I went to school the next day. Mom told me I didn't have to go but I wanted to get away from my house and the grieving faces. Since the day after Emily was killed, Aunt Shari and Uncle Matt spent the night, sleeping in Mom's bed while she slept on the couch. I couldn't look at them anymore. They just reminded me Emily was gone, so I thought going to school would help me forget. But for a reason I could never explain, I took Emily's picture to school with me.

As soon as I walked through the doors, I was met with hundreds of eyes. A lot of them had never glanced in my direction before. Their eyes looked at me knowingly, their mouths tightened, and the corners descended into slight frowns. Some of them cocked their heads to the side. A few hands reached out to brush my shoulder and pat my back. I just looked down at the floor and walked to my locker. I opened its door and Krissa approached me. She reached her arms around me and hugged me sideways.

"I'm so sorry." I saw tears in her eyes. She thrust a folded up piece of notebook paper into my face. "Here." I took the paper and she walked away as quickly as she'd approached. I opened the note. She wrote she couldn't say the words because she didn't want to cry, said how sorry she was Emily had died, and told me she was there for me if I needed her. I folded the paper and pushed it into my jeans pocket. I swallowed the saliva funneling into my mouth and took a deep breath, hoping no one else would hug me. The eyes and sympathetic looks followed me to math class; everyone knew and I just wanted to be invisible.

I went to my seat and laid my head in my arms on the top of the desk until the tardy bell rang. When I looked up, Mr. Munck was drawing triangles on the blackboard. I took Emily's picture from my binder's front cover and stared at it. *What am I doing here?* I thought. *Emily is dead and all Mr. Munck wants to talk about are sines and cosines?* I hated his apparent ignorance as much as I hated all of the staring. I watched the blackboard while my classmates worked on their geometry. The chalk numbers began to blur. I started to cry; tears slipped silently down my face. Mr. Munck picked up the receiver of the phone on the corner of his desk and whispered into it. A few minutes later, the guidance counselor came in; she picked up my books, grabbed my hand, and led me to her office. Mom picked me up to take me home and I spent the rest of the day curled on my bed listening to tapes.

I went back to school on Monday and everyone went back to ignoring me. I took a test, turned in a book report and three math homework assignments, and earned A's on all of them. On Saturday night, I babysat Forti and Prio while

Uncle Matt went out with his friend, Charlie, and Mom and Aunt Shari went to dinner and a movie. I put Forti and Prio to bed at eight and I sat down in front of the TV. I tried to watch the weekly made-for-TV movie, but it just took me back to that last Saturday night when I was trying to get Emily to stay in bed.

Three of the kids in my grade had volunteered and been chosen to be trained as "peer counselors"; Larry Benson was one of them. Using the telephone on the wall in the kitchen, I dialed his number. My heart pounded in my ears and my whole body shook as I listened to the phone ringing through the line.

"Hello, Benson residence." I recognized the voice as Larry's little sister, Shelly.

"Is Larry there?" My voice cracked.

"Hold please." I almost smiled at Shelly's exaggerated politeness. I heard a clunk and faint, "Larry, it's for you."

I almost hung up just before Larry got to the phone. "Hello," he said.

"Hi. This is Ami Sinkey."

"Hi." I waited. "I was wondering if you had a few minutes to talk."

"Not really. I'm watching the Bulls," he said.

I wanted to yell at him but I just hung up. I got angry. *What kind of peer counselor is that?* I decided then I hated Larry Benson.

Somehow the rest of April passed. I busied my mind with school work and hating Larry. When the weather was warm enough, I walked. I loaded jackets with cassettes recorded with my favorite songs and played them on my Walkman. The only concrete things I remember during that time until I got Nada's next letter was staring either at the ceiling or into the river and listening to music. Sometimes I imagined Larry crawling to me, devastated with guilt, and begging my forgiveness. I would begrudgingly give in and then he would become my boyfriend. Mostly I just concentrated on the words in the music I listened to, imagining myself singing them to packed audiences.

*   *   *   *   *

1 May 1991

Dear Ami,

I will try to tell you about what it is like to live in Republic of Croatia in Yugoslavia. I have never been to Serbia. But I am Serb. At least this is what I'm told by my country. The religion of my parents' parents and their parents before them was Catholic Orthodox so my religion is Catholic Orthodox. We are not devout. We attend church mainly on holidays. Most people where I live in Rijeka are Roman Catholic and they are called Croats. I do not know why this is so. I do not know why Catholic Orthodox and Roman Catholic are different. I know at one time they were same religion. They split in year 1054. I do not know why. I know there are some differences in how we do things. Orthodox Catholic churches do not have chairs and our holidays fall on different days. To make the cross on our bodies, Orthodox Catholics use three fingers and go from left to right. Roman Catholics go from right to left with their full hand.

I became a communist when I was seven years old and I was happy. One of the first things we do at school is pledge ourselves to communism during the PRIMANJE U

PIONIRE ceremony. My new classmates and I wore blue pants, white shirts, yellow scarves, and blue berets with red stars on them. We repeated the oath. We sang a Yugoslavian hymn and received red carnations. They gave us pictures of our President, Tito, and cards declaring us parts of the communist party. We were communists but we did not know what a communist was. But we went to school, played, and had families who loved us. We had clothes to wear and food to eat so it was good to be communist. It was a few years before I learned I am a Serb. I am only now beginning to learn it makes a difference.

Homework and school come before anything else in my family. I am in seventh grade so the grades I earn this year and next year in eighth grade will determine the rest of my life. Mama is pleased I have been able to earn all A's so far.

I did not get a letter from you since I wrote my last letter to you. I don't know if it got lost in the mail so I decided to write you again. Please write back soon!

Your Friend,
Nada

Jodie Toohey

CHAPTER SIX

A month passed; I wanted to write Nada but I didn't know what to say. I received another letter from her in June.

*　　*　　*　　*　　*

3 June 1991

Dear Ami,

I do not know if you are writing me or if you are not getting my letters. I don't know if our mail is messed up because of what is happening. I will keep writing until I get something back from you. If you are getting my letters, please write me back.

Have you ever had anything happen that made life seem perfect but later realized it was too perfect and you should have known things would change? This happened to me yesterday. When I was high enough up the hill between school and my house and I could feel it on my back, I turned to face the sea. It was deep blue and pierced by ships docking or departing the harbor. It felt like its breath snuck up the hillside and blew in my face. It was warm and sweet with a hint of salt. My house has three neighbors on one side and four on the other attached in a row, all looking out onto sea. Before I walked through my front door, I turned once more toward the sea. I looked ahead to two weeks to my fourteenth birthday swimming in that very water.

Maja ran up behind me and I pushed the door open wider to let her in. "I didn't know it was a race," I said. I crossed my arms in front of my chest. I was calm, not like Maja. She came in. When she lost her grip on the door, it slammed shut, sucked closed by the pressure from the warm wind cutting through the house. Mama left the windows on back sides of our fourth and fifth stories and front side of our second story open so the sea's wind would enter and rush up the stairs out the back windows. It was so nice to stand there and feel the wind sweep fresh air through my house. I had to force myself to do my homework.

I had just enough time to finish homework and do chores before Tata would be home and it would be time to start cooking supper. Then I would be able to sit down while supper is cooking to watch television instead of returning to school work.

At three o'clock, I put my studies away and began my chores. I swept all of our brown tile and hardwood floors. There seemed to be more dust.

Tata arrived home just before four o'clock. He is a postman and delivers mail for Croatia. He said hello and hugged my sister and me as usual. He was quiet as he began to fry ground beef and cut vegetables. I finished sweeping and returned broom to narrow closet by our back door. I peeled the green outer leaves from a head of cauliflower and began to chop it into bite-size pieces. We made Musaka. It is one of my favorite dishes. The bottom layer is a mixture of cooked onions, ground beef, cauliflower, and tomatoes. It is topped with a layer of sour cream.

Tata didn't ask me about my day at school like he usually does while we prepare supper. I thought he forgot so I tell him about my latest math problems. He nodded but did not seem to listen. After Tata placed Musaka into oven and I finished cleaning up the preparation dishes, I went upstairs to living room. I sat down on floor and watched television.

Mama, disheveled and tired as usual, returned from business suit factory just as the closing credits began rolling across the screen. She, too, seemed unusually quiet as she helped Tata set the table for supper and checked over Maja's homework. Mama remembered to ask us about our days at school but without excitement. I began to wonder if something was going on but the fresh tomatoey taste of Musaka soon made me forget.

Last night, I heard my parents talk in their bed in bedroom below Maja's and mine in anxious whispers. They talked about their votes in the referendum last month, how the majority of people voted opposite, and what it might mean for future of Yugoslavia and Croatia. Before Mama and Tata went to vote in the election, they explained to Maja and me there were many people in Croatia who no longer wished Croatia to be part of communist country of Yugoslavia. I had been a communist since my oath to honor the communist party. They voted for Croatia to stay a part of Yugoslavia but they were in minority. In their bed, Mama and Tata talked about how they do not know what will happen. Because they do not know what is going to happen, they did not want to worry Maja and me.

I did not tell them I saw a news broadcast at end of last April about how mortar shells were fired at the village Vukovar in middle of the night. But I did not worry. Vukovar is on other side of the Republic of Croatia nearly to border between it and the Republic of Serbia. That day when they came home from work, they were in their usual cheerful moods. I remember the air was just beginning to be warmer and the days were growing longer. We took a walk after supper that night. I thought if Mama and Tata did not think it was safe, they would have told us and would have kept us inside after supper. Now I wonder if they are afraid such fighting might extend all the way to Rijeka.

I'm sorry this letter is so long but I needed to tell somebody about what is happening.

Your friend,
Nada

* * * * *

My mom put Nada's letter on my nightstand next to my bed on Friday night before she kissed me goodnight. I had not moved all day and didn't until Saturday morning when I had to get up because my dad insisted on taking us to Camanche's annual town festival.

I took nearly an hour to get dressed and yawned all the way to the park. Kids were running in every direction with mothers and fathers trailing behind futilely attempting to steer them around mud puddles disguised by flattened, overgrown grass. Each one of the two dozen carnival rides played competing music and my head pounded. It was cloudy and cooler than it had been, but the air was thick and I couldn't pull in enough oxygen.

Dad walked up to the ticket booth. "Three all-day wrist bands, please."

"No, just two," I stood on my toes to see the kid in the booth over Dad's shoulder.

"What?" my dad said.

"I don't want one."

"Why not?"

"I just don't."

"Just two, I guess." He wrapped the paper bands around Forti and Prio's wrists. "Stand still." He barely got the ends stuck together and they ran off toward the Ferris wheel, hand in hand. "Come right back here when the ride's over."

I followed them to the Ferris wheel line.

"Ami," Dad said.

I turned around and squinted the diffused sunlight out of my eyes.

"Ami."

I rolled my eyes and shrugged. "What?"

"Ami, what is the matter with you?"

"*What?*"

"You used to love coming to the carnival and riding all of the rides. Now you are always so quiet and you don't want to do anything. I just don't know what has gotten into you."

"Are you *kidding* me? You don't know what is wrong with me?" I turned and walked away, splashing into a mud puddle.

"Ami." He grabbed my shoulder. "You need to stop dwelling on Emily's death."

"*Dwelling?* In case you can't read a calendar, Dad, she died less than three months ago! How can you tell me that? Just because you left and don't care anymore, it doesn't mean everyone else doesn't care."

"I just meant you need to move on with your life. Go out with friends. Have some fun. Don't mope around all the time."

"Don't tell me what to do! If I'm so hard to be around, why did you even *bring* me here? Emily was my favorite cousin! I spent every Saturday night with her. She was a *baby*. How can you tell me to forget about her? Sorry, Dad, but obviously, I can't forget about family as easily as you can!"

I sat on a park bench for the rest of the day. Occasionally, Forti and Prio took a break from riding rides to sit next to me or hug me. Dad seemed to pretend I wasn't there.

By Monday, I felt worse about not writing to Nada. I didn't want to be selfish, but I didn't know how to explain Emily's death in words. It had been eleven weeks since Emily died. It was obvious the world was not going to stop turning without her, even though it seemed impossible it should. But it wasn't Nada's fault. I thought about how I'd feel if I'd kept writing her but she didn't write me back so I did the best I could.

* * * * *

June 10, 1991

Dear Nada,

I am so sorry it has taken me so long to write back. On March 25th, my favorite little cousin, Emily, died. She was hit by a car when my aunt was pushing her home from the park in her stroller. So I have not known what I should write to you, but I will try to answer the questions in your last letter.

School in America is the same time every day. I go to school from 8:00 a.m. to 3:00 p.m. Mondays through Fridays. Once in a while, I have homework but I have a class we call study hall where I usually finish all of my homework. I walk to school also but it is not very far away, so it is not a long walk. I started school at kindergarten when I was five years old but I turned six years old early in the year so I was six for most of kindergarten. My school usually starts around August 20th and ends at the end of May or the beginning of June. It depends on how many snow days we have to make up. Do you have snow days in Croatia? Snow days here are when the weather is too bad to go to school and usually the bad weather is a lot of snow. Sometimes we also get snow days when we get freezing rain or when the temperature is below zero.

My birthday is September 3, 1976. So you get a birthday gift of getting out of school and I get the birthday gift of going to school.

Larry Benson is a jerk and I do not remember why I liked him. After Emily died, I tried to talk to him about it, but he ignored me. So now I hate him. I don't think there are any boys in America (none that I know anyway) like your Mate. Boys here do not ride motorcycles and they are only nice to girls if they are super popular or their friends are not around them.

I am sorry about the fighting in your country. I hope no fighting has happened by your house and if it has, I'm very sorry. I'm also sorry this letter is so dull. I will try to write more later.

Your friend,
Ami

P.S. Happy Birthday!!

CHAPTER SEVEN

Nada was much better at responding to my letters than I was to hers.

*   *   *   *   *

18 June 1991

Dear Ami,

I got your letter yesterday, right on my birthday! I am sorry your cousin died. That is very, very sad. No fighting has happened by my house since I wrote my last letter but people are saying Yugoslavia may be going to war. I heard on television over 90% of people voted last month in election that they wanted Croatia to be its own country.

I hope by the time you get this letter you are feeling better. Do you want to hear about my birthday and plans for the summer? If you do, keep reading. If not, you can put this

47

letter away and read it later. In case you decide to read rest of this letter later, please write me back when you want to.

My fourteenth birthday was yesterday so Maja and I spent the whole day until it got dark out swimming in the sea with our friends. I am happy it is summer. I do not have to think about grades or homework or studies for almost three months. I am having my birthday party on Saturday afternoon. I will spend most of the rest of my summer riding bicycles, swimming in the sea, and hiking with my friends. In one month, my family will go to visit my mother's parents in Bosnia. I love to feed the chickens, take the cows to pasture, and help my grandmother garden. They grow bushels and bushels of vegetables. We get to feast on as many as we like while we are visiting.

*   *   *   *   *

Nada's letter continued under a different date:

*   *   *   *   *

23 June 1991

Yesterday, I got up early to prepare small sandwiches made out of sourdough bread and different meats and cheeses for my birthday party. We also drank juice and ate cake. My friends arrived right on the time. I wore new blue jeans, new bright white sneakers, and a pink shirt that buttoned down the front. I snapped a barrette into one side of my hair. Sanja said I looked good and I said I hoped Mate thinks so, too. All of my friends came: Sanja, Igor, Zlatko, Ema, Danijela, Ana, Sanjan, Valentina, Helena, Drazen,

Nebojsa, Marko, Mile, Ante, Sandro, Dinjo, Karlo, and, of course, Mate. Mate was the last to arrive. He parked his motorcycle on side of street, kicked the kickstand down to hold it up, and walked toward the door. He wore blue jeans, tennis shoes, and a blue and white striped shirt. His hair was fluffy and bounced as he walked toward me. I held the door open for him and he grinned at me.

"Happy Birthday!" he said.

"Thank you," I said.

When everyone ate enough sandwiches and juice, I turned on music and we started to dance. A slow song began to play and I clasped my hands behind Mate's neck. He reached his hands behind my back and pushed them into the back pockets of my jeans. I ignored Sanja and the others gossiping. I hoped the song would last a long time. When the song ended I looked up into Mate's eyes just a few inches higher than mine. He leaned down and kissed me on the lips, soft and long. The second my arms dropped back to my sides, Sanja grabbed my arm and pulled me toward the bathroom.

"Girl stuff," she said to Mate. When she got me in the bathroom and closed the door, she made me describe every detail of the kiss.

After we danced, we played a game where we turn the lights off and one of us tries to find the others in the dark. That was so fun and we were all laughing and falling into each other. Too soon, Mama turned the lights back on and it was time for everyone to go home. It was a great party. Will you have a party for your birthday?

Write me back when you can!

Your friend,
Nada

*   *   *   *   *

Following Nada's lead, I wrote her back the day I received her letter.

*   *   *   *   *

July 1, 1991

Dear Nada,

Your birthday party sounds fun. Congratulations on Mate! (Wink, wink.) I am still waiting for my first kiss so you are way ahead of me.

I miss Emily a lot. It still doesn't seem possible that she is dead. Every day, I am going through life without her, but I still can't imagine how life is going to be without her. Isn't that weird? Can I tell you a secret? My mom and my family think I am okay. My mom, grandparents, Aunt Shari, and Uncle Matt (Emily's parents) have been through so much that I want to be strong for them. Forti and Prio are so much work for my mom, I try my hardest to be good and be as easy as I can. I smile, laugh, and play with Forti and Prio. I walk or ride my bike to the library every other day and come home with armloads of books to read. I tell my family I am studying so I can go to college one day because I don't want to end up like my mom, which has taught me I cannot depend on a husband or anyone else to reach my goals. But really I read to forget. My secret is my family thinks I am fine, but I'm not. I lie awake in my bed at night, sometimes until it is almost getting light out, with memories of Emily and Larry and other horrible thoughts bombarding my brain. And it starts to feel like something heavy is pushing down on my chest. I think I will stop breathing. I cannot stop crying but eventually I fall asleep. The funny thing is, when I wake up, the night before seems like it was all a dream and I actually think I will be better. But then the night comes, I go to bed, and everything comes back.

When I go to the library, it only takes me a little while to find the books I want to check out. I am not in a hurry to go home so I sit on the pier that sticks out into the river. There are benches and a cement slab down some stairs where boats can tie up and come to shore. Yesterday, I sat on that cement slab and I thought about jumping into the river. I didn't want to die. I just wanted to float away down to the Gulf of Mexico. I was jealous of the water rushing past me and away on its journey. I was jealous because the river never stays in one place; it is always moving and never becomes attached to anything or anyone. I think if I could not be attached to anyone or anything, it would not hurt me when they leave.

I hope you do not find this letter too depressing to read. I do not have anyone else to "talk" to but I feel a little better just putting it on paper. Please write back soon!

Your friend,
Ami

CHAPTER EIGHT

Though I started writing to Nada on July 1st, I couldn't find the motivation to finish my letter until Independence Day. Not wanting to make her wait any longer, I decided to walk it to the box at the post office so it could get going right away when they opened again on July 5th.

When I told her my plans, my mom said, "Will you take Forti and Prio with you? I'm trying to get the picnic ready for the fireworks tonight and they won't stay out of my way."

"But they are so slow," I said.

"Let Forti ride her bike and pull Prio in the wagon."

"Okay."

I pulled the wagon from the dark corner of the garage onto the driveway and called Forti and Prio outside.

"Mom wants me to take you with me to the post office. Forti, get your bike. Prio, you ride in the wagon." I lifted Prio onto the dusty red plastic seat.

Forti wrinkled her nose as she looked at the wagon's cup holder. "Eww, that's gross." I twisted to make sure Nada's letter was secure in my back pocket. Forti screamed. I thought she fell off of her bike. She pointed at the wagon. "Spider!"

Prio jumped over the side of the wagon. He sprung up and brushed his hands together.

"Knock it off. It's just a spider. You're scaring Prio." Prio stood with his arms folded. "It's okay; get back in," I said. His eyes were big as he shook his head. "Fine. We'll wash it off. Go in and get a wet towel."

Forti didn't respond but just laid her bike down. She came back and I wiped all of the dust, spider webs, and spiders from the wagon. When Prio was finally satisfied after inspecting the wagon top to bottom, he got in.

The sun was hot and made my forehead sweat. The weather was typical for the Fourth of July. I remembered it had been hotter and cooler in past years. As I pulled the wagon over the cracked sidewalks, I thought about Emily. I should've been pulling her with Prio in the wagon and getting ready for the fireworks with her. I wondered if she would have been old enough to like them now or if they would have just scared her. Forti was scared of fireworks until last year. He'd cry and try to crawl into Mom's neck. Then, last year, he giggled every time he heard the boom when they were shot from the ground. I thought, *Now I will never know*, and my throat started to close as I tried to suppress my tears.

As I pulled down the collection box door, I heard Forti shout, "Shelly!"

I turned around; Forti ran across the street without looking. The lump in my throat turned from tears to panic. I scanned the street; luckily, the closest car was two blocks away. "Forti, you could've been killed. What are you doing?"

"Just a minute." Forti pulled up to Shelly.

"Come on! I'm ready to go."

She turned, gave me a dirty look, and held up her index finger. I sighed as loud as I could and glared at her with my hands on my hips. Larry walked up from around the corner. He looked straight at me but didn't try to talk to me or even wave. He whispered something in Shelly's ear and then he looked everywhere but at me; the sky, the house next to him, and the bank across the street. I stared at him but he still didn't look back. *I should just go over there and punch him*, I thought. But I was afraid he might hit me back.

"Forti!"

"I'm coming," she said. She straddled her bike and pointed the front tire toward the middle of the street.

"Watch for cars!"

"I am!" She whipped her head from side to side, stood on her pedals, and rode across the street. She sped ahead of us toward home.

"I'm telling mom," I yelled at her back.

She hollered into the sky, "Not if I tell her first!"

I looked back at Prio and shook my head. He copied me but his head made more of a circle. I smiled a little.

* * * * *

10 July 1991

Dear Ami,

Your secrets are safe with me. If it helps you to feel better by writing me what is happening to you, please keep doing it. Promise me you will not jump into your river!

Please do not be worried if you do not get a letter from

me in quite a while. I may be moving. Croatia declared itself independent from Yugoslavia on 25 June. They are going to make Tata join the Croatian army. Tata does not want to go into army. As I wrote before, most people where I live in Croatia are Roman Catholic and are called Croats. Only our closest friends know we are Serb. In other parts of Croatia, the majority of people are Serb. Serbs make up the Yugoslav army. They want to keep Yugoslavia together while the Croats want to make Croatia its own country. If Tata is forced to join the Croatian army, he will be made to kill people from his own religion. Also, we hear about Serbs who have been forced to join the Croatian army who are killed by that very same army. But army tells the family he has been killed by Serbs. My parents are now always talking about what to do. They are deciding if we should all move to Italy or if Tata should leave and go to Italy. I do not know what will happen. I also do not sleep much at night wondering what will happen.

One thing I do know is going to happen is war is coming to Croatia. It may already be here. Serbs and Croats are fighting. We used to live side by side. We used to be friends. Now they are saying Serbs must go to Serbia and Croats must come to Croatia. But Serbia is not my home.

My parents told us we will not be going to Bosnia to visit my grandparents this summer. People were fighting between Rijeka and their village. It would dangerous to attempt to pass through it. Besides, they don't know where we will be or what we will be doing by then. Since Croatia declared itself an independent country from Yugoslavia, Tata has been sick with worry. He has received calls in middle of nearly every night, some at 2 a.m. and some at 3 a.m. They are from his work ordering him to deliver letters from the Croatian army to men nearby. The letters say those men must serve. Tata knows his letter is coming one day. He does not know what to do.

The fighting between Croats and Serbs is becoming more intense. Four days ago, the town of Celije between Osijek and Vinkovci was burned and Croats in Osijek harassed Serb citizens so much they fled the town for surrounding villages where there are more Serbs. Three days ago, Serb civilians and Croatian police fought for more than eight hours. It seems so far away but I am still afraid. I am afraid the fighting will march across Croatia to Rijeka.

Mama and Tata have had hushed conversations every night since Croatia declared its independence on 25 June. Tata has almost stopped eating because everything he eats causes his stomach to burn. He saw his doctor on Friday who said he had an ulcer caused by worry and stress. They talked about selling our house and leaving, but where would we go? They worked hard to buy this house when I was nine years old. They don't want to leave it. When everything settles back down, they do not want to be forced to start over. Tata cannot risk going into Croatian army.

Last night, their discussion continued. I tried my best to stay awake while I listened. Finally, after several moments of silence, Mama said, "So it is decided then?"

"Yes," said Tata.

"You will go to Italy to work?"

Tata did not answer but the silence between them signaled his agreement. What will we do without Tata? In my entire fourteen years, my father has not spent one night away from our family. I strained my ears hoping there was more. I hoped that was not the end of the conversation and not the final decision. I do not know what I want final decision to be. I do not want Tata to go to war and I do not want to leave our beautiful home. There must be another option. I listened myself into exhaustion and finally slept.

I am sorry I have jumped all around in this letter. I feel I no longer know what to think. Ami, I am afraid, but like you, I do not want to worry Mama or Tata. They have too much to worry about already. Maybe we can keep writing to each other and it will help.

Please write back soon.

Your Friend,
Nada

CHAPTER NINE

I hoped Nada was right. I wasn't sure how I could help her live through war. But it helped me feel a little better just knowing I had a friend somewhere who cared. Maybe I could help by just making Nada know that I was her friend.

*   *   *   *   *

July 16, 1991

Dear Nada,

I have not heard about a war in Croatia. Maybe there was something, but I missed it. Our world news is mostly about Kuwait, the Gulf War, and the Soviet Union. I was shopping at a store when it came on the news America was at war in Saudi Arabia. It was Wednesday, January 16, 1991; I kept our newspaper from that day because there had not been a war during my lifetime. I remember I thought it felt really weird being at war because history was going on, and people were getting killed, but life was going on as usual. It felt strange to be studying, going to the store, and going to school when my country was at war. But then all of the fighting was not happening in my country; it was on the other side of the world, so I knew I was safe. Some kids from school had brothers and uncles fighting in the war so I was concerned about them, of course, but I knew I was safe from the war in my home. I can't imagine how weird it must be to have war fighting right in your own country.

The summer is so long. It is hot and I am bored. All I do is sleep. I do not feel like doing anything. I try to read, but after I read a few pages, I cannot remember what I read. After I start over three or four times, I give up and put the book away. I sit in my bedroom listening to music and crying. When my mom stops to see if I am okay, I put the book in front of my face so she cannot see my tears and I tell her I am fine. I lie.

*   *   *   *   *

I tried to write about something happier for Nada. She was in the middle of war and I was sure she didn't want to hear more depressing thoughts. But I became frustrated and crossed the words out. I tried again as tension flowed to my hand, crippling it from writing another word. The heat in my room seemed to rise. I went downstairs to get a glass of water. Forti and Prio were playing outside in the sprinkler. I grabbed the water and hurried back to my room before they or my mom saw me. I sat back down at my desk, took a drink, and felt the cold dripping into my stomach. I picked up my pen again. I tried to write something better but the only thing coming out was dark. The words spilled out and filled the rest of the page and the familiar hell crept in. My body flushed, taken over by the feeling of hopelessness. I held my breath, willing the air from my lungs to force itself against my skull until I became dizzy and saw sparkling lights in front of my eyes. Suddenly enraged, I balled my half-finished letter and threw it across my room. It hit the wall and dropped to the floor.

When I stood up, I knocked over my water; the clear liquid flowed across the surface of my desk and dripped off the edge. I backed away like it would overtake and drown me. The knob on my bedroom door halted my retreat and I crumbled to the floor. I looked around my blurry room and desperately reached for peace. I sat curled on my floor for hours and waited. Vicious voices assaulted me saying my life was miserable, I was miserable, and I was a failure, but they eventually wore themselves out. I tried to remember a time when I felt okay. I used a t-shirt from my dirty clothes hamper to wipe up the partially dried water. I picked up my crumpled letter and smoothed it on my desk. I turned it over and wrote:

*　*　*　*　*

I'm sorry if I do not make much sense. I am not myself lately, but then again, who is that? I hope this letter finds you safe and sound. I am sending my best wishes to you with this letter.

Your friend,
Ami

* * * * *

After I placed the letter into the mailbox, I shaded my eyes as I studied the front door. The sidewalk felt like miles. Suddenly, I wanted to lie down on the grass and fall asleep. I pushed the front door closed. It was heavy, like it was constructed from bricks.

"Ami, what do you want for lunch?" Mom called from somewhere in the back of the house.

"I'm not hungry."

My mom appeared. She wiped her hands on a towel. Her hair was pulled into a bun and a handkerchief was tied around her head. "Are you sure? I'm almost done canning the last batch of tomatoes. Forti and Prio will need to eat; I'm surprised they aren't in here screaming they're hungry already."

"I'm sure. I think I want to take a nap."

"Are you feeling okay?"

"I just feel really tired," I said.

Her smile told me she was letting me go because she didn't want to argue.

I vaguely remembered a sliver of light cutting through the darkness between the bedroom door and jamb. When I awoke the next morning, the day before felt like a dream. I had to think hard before convincing myself I had mailed Nada her letter. The attack I suffered while writing the letter felt unreal; like it happened years rather than hours ago. I kept thinking about Nada. When I received her next letter, I was more convinced our lives were very similar even though they were so different.

*   *   *   *   *

26 July 1991

Dear Ami,

It is Wednesday. Tata left for Italy in middle of the night. He quit his job as a postman on Monday and packed his bags on Tuesday. He wants to find a place to stay in Verona, Italy, so he can begin to look for work right away on Monday. Early this morning when night had barely faded to its early morning soft blue, I swallowed the tears rising in my throat as I replayed hugging Tata in middle of the night before he drove away in his car. He usually gets a new used car every year to fix up and sell. He just finished fixing up this latest one, a Yugo, a couple of weeks ago. He and Mama promised everything will be all right. I believe them but do not know how anything can be all right with my family torn apart.

I could not sleep so I sat in front of my house. I looked down the road where hours before we watched Tata drive away until his car dropped into valley out of our sight. My neighbor, Marko, came out his front door on his way to work as I turned back toward our house. I smiled and waved but he focused his eyes on his car parked on the side of the street like I was not there. We are learning more and more we are becoming less popular in our neighborhood. I saw on television news Croats were kicked out and crimes were committed against them in Dalj, Erdut, Aljmas, and other places in the Slavonia part of eastern Croatia. Though the news has not mentioned it, Mama heard at work Serbs have been harassed by authorities in some places so much they fled to areas with higher Serb populations.

As soon as I got back in the house, Mama, behind schedule, grabbed her lunch and rushed to work. I watched television for a while and then called Sanja on telephone. I love to use the black telephone on its own shelf that sticks out from the wall in our living room. I like to turn the dial and listen to whirring noise it makes as it returns to its original position. Phone numbers with eights and nines in them are most fun. We also have a red telephone in kitchen we received free from buying laundry soap that looks a little like red lips, but it just uses push buttons.

After I hung up from talking with Sanja, I removed my bicycle from the garage on the bottom floor of our house. I waited for her so we could ride. Sanja has been my friend as long as I can remember. She is Roman Catholic, only because her parents and grandparents were Roman Catholic just like the reason I am Catholic Orthodox. Other than to wish each other "Merry Christmas" on our own holidays, we do not talk about religion.

I saw Sanja drive her bike up the hill. She waved with one hand and wobbly steered her bike as she strained to propel herself up the steep incline. By this scene, one would never know people others have deemed "our people" are killing each other.

Sanja and I don't care about the war. At least I don't care when we are together. We spent day riding side by side up and down the streets of our neighborhood. We stopped only for lunch. We sat on side of the street and removed our lunches from the wrinkled brown paper bags we packed them in at home. I ate my ham, cheese, bell pepper, and tomato sandwich while Sanja ate hers. After lunch, Maja tore herself away from the television to join us.

We rode to Mate's house to see if he wanted to come

along. The sun, without any clouds to block it, beat hot on my head. The air was still except for an occasional wave of salty breeze brushing over the hills. It was Maja's idea to go see Mate. I think she likes Mate but I am not worried. Mate likes Maja but just as a little sister. Mate lives several blocks from my neighborhood. His house shares no walls with his neighbors. It is smaller inside than mine. Sanja, Maja, and I laid our bikes on their sides against the curb on the side of the street. I led our little group to door. Stepping onto stoop, I smoothed my hair away from my face. Before I rang the doorbell, I turned to Sanja and asked her if I looked all right.

"You look fine." Maja reached around my shoulders and pushed doorbell. Mate's closed windows muffled the musical "ding-dong" but we could still hear it. I heard heavy footsteps approaching the door from somewhere toward the back of house. Mate's mother peeked through the curtains hiding the windows in brown front door. I smiled and waved. She peeked through again and bit her lip. For a moment, I wondered if she was even going to open the door, but then I heard the click of door's lock and the door, swollen from the summer air, lurched open.

"Hi, Mrs. Jaksic. Is Mate home?" Something didn't seem right about Mate's mother. I did not mention it and just smiled.

"No," was all she said. We waited for more explanation and then I saw Mate few feet behind the door.

"Hi Mate." I waved. Mate looked at the floor.

With her voice shaking, Mrs. Jaksic said, "I mean he's here but he can't come to door. He isn't feeling well."

"Okay. Can we say hello?"

"No, you'd better not." Mate's mother pulled door open wider and turned to Mate. "Go lay back down, Mate." Mate didn't move. He just stood there staring at his mother. He seemed like he wanted to speak but just as he opened his mouth, his mother snapped, "Tell them you are not feeling well, Mate." I recognized the look she gave him. It is the same look my parents give me when they want me to do exactly what they tell me to do, no more and no less.

Mate folded his arms on his chest. He squinted his eyes at his mother then turned them to me and said gently, "I'm not feeling well."

Before I could say "I hope you feel better soon," the door closed and Mate was gone.

"What was that all about?" Sanja strained to see into Mate's house through the curtains.

"I don't know. Let's go," I said. But I think I do know. Mate's family's religion is Roman Catholic and most of the Roman Catholic adults I know have been behaving strange lately.

At four o'clock, we returned home to start supper. After working all day sewing business suits in the hot factory, Maja and I know Mama will appreciate our efforts. Mama didn't instruct us to start this task but Tata, when he was telling us to be good for Mama, asked us to help out wherever we could, especially those things Tata usually did. Tata always cooked supper before Mama returned from work so we did the same.

On our way inside, I used our mailbox key to remove our mail from our metal mailbox stuck on the side of our house. I placed it in a neat stack on the kitchen table for Mama to see. I used to flip through the mail hoping to get a letter or a party invitation, but last week, Mama and Tata told us not to look at the mail anymore. I had no hint as to why until I saw Mama's face fall as she read a letter she received earlier today.

She pulled out the chair nearest to stack of mail. The metal legs scraped on floor. She held the mail on end and flipped through them like recipe cards. She stopped quick and the pieces of mail in front and behind the one that caught her attention dropped flat on table. She held toward the light a long narrow envelope, the same size as the ones our bills arrive in but without the clear plastic window. She turned it over. There was no return address, just our printed name and address on the front like anyone could have written it. I noticed her hands shake as she unfolded the paper. She noticed me watching her as I stirred the boiling onion, sugar, red peppers, and tomatoes for our Sataraš on stove. It was boiling a long time and smelled good.

Mama forced a smile and said, "How are you doing over there?"

I was embarrassed she caught me staring at her so I mumbled, "Fine," and focused on the cooking. I thought it must be a short letter as Mama quickly folded the paper, returned it to envelope, and stuffed it in a kitchen drawer.

"Anything interesting in the mail?" I asked.

"No, just the usual bills. Nothing to be concerned about." I knew she was lying but I didn't argue. We can feel Tata's absence, but somehow, he seems more present away than he did when he was here. Mama smiled and excused herself to bathroom, but I saw tears in her eyes. Later, when Mama was occupied in her shower, I quietly retrieved the letter from its hiding place. I read: *GET OUT. GO BACK TO SERBIA OR BE KILLED.*

This is all letter said. It was typewritten, the letters wobbly from the smear of the ink on the typewriter ribbon. It was not dated or signed. It did not say "Dear" anyone. It just said to get out or be killed. My hands trembled as I folded the letter, returned it to envelope, and the place in the drawer with the other mail Mama is saving to show Tata. I do not know why, but when I opened the drawer to replace the letter, I lifted the other papers in the drawer and found two other envelopes addressed like the one I just read. I quietly removed them, unfolded them, and read similar threats. One said, *ALL SERBS SHALL DIE*, and the other, *IF YOU DO NOT LEAVE, WE WILL COME IN THE MIDDLE OF THE NIGHT TO SLIT YOUR THROATS.*

I heard the splats of shower water hitting the bathtub floor stop. Mama was done and I had only a few moments to return the letters to where I found them.

Before I started writing this letter, I was lying in bed thinking about those letters. I did not tell Maja about them. I did not want to scare her and I could not tell Mama without getting in trouble for reading the mail after I was told not to read it. I keep thinking about who could have sent the letters. Do they know my family? Do they know Tata is away in Italy? Was it one of the neighbors who no longer greets us when we see them coming home from work? Was it one person who sent the letters? Two or three?

It is warm in our bedroom but I cannot stop shivering. Mama left our window open to let in fresh, summer evening air. When I was in bed, the curtains wavered only slightly from wind, but it felt like they were whispering to me. I jumped out of bed, shut and latched the window, but didn't look outside. I was too afraid of what I might see. I clutched my blankets to my chin and lay flat on my back so I could see in all directions except for the wall behind my head. I held my breath every time I heard a noise. I heard Maja sigh, the creak of floor, and the trees outside my window. I held my breath until tiny lights sparkled in front of my eyes, and then I sucked in deep. I watched the shadows and thought they were coming. I tried to plan my escape. If they came in the door, I would grab Maja and go out window. If they came in the window, I would grab Maja, run for Mama, and leave the house. But where would we go?

I got out of bed and started writing this letter.

(Continued next morning.) Sometime before dawn, sleep overpowered my fear. When I awoke, the room was bright and my window was open. I looked over to Maja's bed but it was empty. My throat closed. I wondered just a fraction of a second why they didn't take me when I heard the high-pitched cartoon voices from the television in the living room downstairs. I got up, dressed, and made my bed. I made Maja's bed thinking she'd owe me and I'd collect when it was time to clean the house later. I found Maja giggling at the television just like any other day.

Your Friend,
Nada

Jodie Toohey

CHAPTER TEN

I wondered what I could say to Nada to make her feel better. I had heard stories of robbers breaking into houses in the middle of the night and killing families, but it either happened so far away or the robbers were looking for something they knew the family had. They didn't break into kill them because they went to the wrong church.

*　*　*　*　*

July 31, 1991

Dear Nada,

I am sorry your dad had to go work in Italy and I am sorry about Mate. I wish there was something I could write to make you feel better, but I can't think of anything. I hope everything turns out okay and you stay safe.

Last week, I had a dream Emily was still alive. I saw her face in my dream the way it was; all smiles and blue eyes. It is getting harder for me to picture her face in my mind when I am awake, but she was so real in my dream. My Aunt Shari brought her to my house and she ran to me as soon as Aunt Shari put her down on the floor. I hugged her, picked her up, and then I started crying hard. I felt myself waking up and I tried to stay asleep, but I woke up anyway. My pillow was wet. Every night since then, I wish I would dream of Emily again, but I haven't.

Next month, I have to go stay with my dad and Nikki for a whole week. I am not looking forward to it. When we go visit every other weekend, both of them treat all of us like we are Prio's age, and Dad and Nikki are always touching each other. It makes me want to puke. I don't know if I will be able to make it there for an entire week.

I have less than a month until I go back to school and I can't wait. I am so bored with summer. It is hot outside. I just stay inside all day reading books or lying on my floor listening to music. When the sun starts to go down, I go for a walk and sit by the river. Sometimes I still think about jumping in, but I promise I won't without telling you first.

I am sorry this letter is boring; I don't have much to say. But since any excitement is probably going to be bad excitement, I guess I'd rather take boring. I hope you are feeling better and your dad gets to come home soon. Write back when you can!

Your friend,

Ami

*   *   *   *   *

I looked out my window. The mail truck was coming down the street. I raced down the stairs to put a stamp on my letter, hoping I could make it to the mailbox in time. A strange noise stopped me halfway between the living room and kitchen. It sounded like a muffled dog barking. I peeked around the kitchen wall, "Mom?"

She sat slumped over the kitchen table, her forehead resting on top of her folded hands. "Mom?" I asked again. She looked up. Her eyes were rimmed in red; she wiped them with the back of her hand. I looked around for Prio and Forti but didn't see them. A bit of panic crept into my throat.

"Mom, what's wrong?"

"Nothing. I was just cutting onions." I neither saw nor smelled any evidence of onions. "What are you doing?"

"I was getting stamps so I can mail a letter to my pen pal."

"You'd better hurry. I think the mail truck is at the neighbor's." I looked at my mom but she said nothing else. I ran out the door to give my letter directly to the mail carrier. When I came back in, I went to my bedroom, lay on my bed, and cried.

*   *   *   *   *

8 August 1991

Dear Ami,

I am still at my home in Rijeka. Tata is working in Italy as a welder. His company makes excavation tools like loader and backhoe buckets. He has been away for almost two weeks. He won't be able to come home for a visit for a couple more weeks. I am sad because we will not be able to make trip to Bosnia to visit my grandparents this summer. There is fighting between here and there so it is too dangerous. Besides, Tata has to work since this is a new job. Mama still works at the suit factory. Maja and I still ride bicycles, swim in the sea, and play with our friends, but I am scared.

I am scared and I have no one to talk to. I do not sleep at night but just lay in bed waiting. I'm not sure what I am waiting for. I suppose I am waiting for daylight because daytime is when everything is okay. Have you seen anything on your television yet? It is a war here. The Sunday before Tata left for Italy, there was fighting in eastern Croatia between Serb people and Croatian police officers. My parents have received more letters telling us to leave or we will be killed, but since I am forbidden from looking at the mail when it arrives, I cannot tell my parents I know about letters.

It is not a good place to be a Serb right now. Some of our neighbors will not even look at us when we walk right by them. It is like they think my family is personally trying to block Croatia from being independent. I have not seen Mate as much lately. He told me his parents forbid him to see me because I am a Serb, but he sneaks to my house on his motorcycle when he can. We cannot go for rides anymore because someone will see him and tell his parents. It is the middle of summer and even with everything happening, we go to beach almost every day. On the weekends, Mama, Maja, and I still go hiking.

Do you still hate your Larry Benson? Do you have your eye on someone new? I hope everything is better for you.

Please write me back when possible.

Your friend,
Nada

*   *   *   *   *

I folded Nada's letter and filed it in my saved box of other letters, cards, and mementos. I could not imagine living in a country with an actual war happening. How scary it would be to lie in bed at night wondering if someone is going to come in to kill you.

"Ami, he's here!" Forti yelled at me from the bottom of the stairs. We were going to spend a week with my dad and Nikki at their new house. I stuffed some paper and an envelope in my duffle bag to write Nada back. I hoisted it onto my shoulder and went downstairs. Forti and Prio were jumping up and down, hugging Dad. I didn't want to go; I didn't want to leave my mom alone. Since the day she lied about the onions, I hadn't caught her crying, but several times, she came out of the bathroom with red rims around her eyes. She told me I had to go because she worried about Prio and Forti and I needed to look after them. If I didn't go, they couldn't go, but they wanted to go to the zoo and the park like Dad promised.

"There's my Amicus Lambicus!" I rolled my eyes. My dad hadn't called me that since I was three years old. He reached his hand toward my head but I ducked away.

"Hi, Dad."

Nikki stood behind Dad, her hands tucked into a crisp, pale yellow trench coat, even though there were only three clouds in the entire sky.

"You remember Nikki?" my dad said.

How could I forget Nikki? I thought. Her make-up made me think she was confused; like she was expecting to meet a political dignitary or Oscar winner rather than her sugar-daddy's three kids. Her hair was perfect; each strand carefully arranged to be stylish, but just out of place enough to remind the world she was young and hip. I thought it likely she used more hairspray in one day than my mother used in her entire life. But I guess if what Dad likes are perfectly imperfect-haired trophies, my mom deserved better anyway.

Nikki crouched down like she was summoning a puppy, "Hi Ami! I'm so excited to spend time with you. I thought we could have a spa day, get our hair done, and do our nails. How does that sound?" Her voice was high and mousy.

I thought about informing her I was not five years old, but instead waved my stub-nailed fingers in front of her. "I don't have any nails to do," I said, but she didn't get it.

"Oh, that's all right; we'll just stick with the hair then." She stood back up, tilted her head, and gave me an empty grin. Now I felt even more like a puppy; one who you just realized will take more training than you had thought, but you cannot be angry with it because, after all, it is just a puppy.

My mom hugged Prio, Forti, and then me. She whispered, "Be polite," in my ear.

Forti and Prio chatted with my dad and Nikki all the way to their new house, which was bigger than our own. Nikki curtseyed and waved us inside.

"Isn't it adorable?" she said. "We had it professionally decorated." A white couch faced a gas fireplace and a blue throw blanket was arranged over the arm. Perfectly imperfect. My dad sat on the couch and patted the cushion next to him.

"Where am I sleeping?" I asked.

"I'll show you in a couple of minutes. Why don't you come sit down? We can catch up and decide what we want to do this week."

"I'm really tired. Can I just take a nap?"

Nikki clapped her hands. "Of course you can." She took my hand and led me up the stairs to a guest room. I shut the door behind me, pretending I didn't see Nikki standing there. I lay down on top of the covers on the bed, feeling righteous and ashamed. After a few minutes, I heard Prio, Forti, Nikki, and Dad laughing down the stairs. I took my paper and pen from my duffle bag, turned onto my side, and wrote Nada back.

*   *   *   *   *

August 16, 1991

Dear Nada,

I hope you are okay. Once in a while they show the fighting on the news and it looks horrible. I have not heard any mention of fighting in Rijeka so I am hopeful you are safe. I cannot imagine living in a country where there is fighting of war. Do you have to stay inside your house all day yet? Have you still been able to ride your bike or see your friends? I hope you are not too bored.

I am supremely bored. I am at my dad's and nitwit-Nikki's new house this week. We just got here. My dad and Nikki have promised to go to all of the places and do all of the things he ever casually mentioned we would do when he became a doctor. It is like he just remembered he had kids.

Forti and Prio are so happy because Dad and Nikki usually buy them everything they act even remotely interested in. Guilt gifts; that's what they are. Forti and Prio may be bought, but I am not for sale. Don't get me wrong; I like gifts as much as anyone else and I'm not going to turn them down, but it doesn't mean I'm going to suddenly forget everything he has done. Do you know what I mean?

Emily will be gone five months on the 25th. It is getting harder and harder to picture her in my mind. Every time I try to think about what her face looked like, the image is not her, but just a photograph I remember seeing. The only image I can remember which is not a photograph is her little lifeless body in her casket. I can't wait to go back to school; at least then I will have something else to think about.

I also cannot wait for next Sunday when I can go back home to my own room and my own bed. I am never able to sleep when I'm not at home. I hope Forti and Prio get enough sleep or I won't be able to stand them. All they will do is whine and complain. It is sometimes hard for me to be a big sister. Is it ever difficult for you to be a big sister?

My school starts in a little more than one week. I really want to get a boyfriend this year. I have been developing a plan of action if I find a boy I become interested in. I am going to do something different by playing it cool and pretending I just want to be friends. So step one is to casually smile and say, "Hi," to him. I am still working on steps two, three, four, etc.

I hope everything is well with you. Write me back when you can.

Your friend,
Ami

Jodie Toohey

CHAPTER ELEVEN

I hadn't realized how much I'd actually looked forward to going to my dad's until it was over and I became more depressed. The Thursday before school started, I was finally able to get out for a walk and be by myself. Even though I had been surrounded by people almost constantly over the past of couple of weeks, I still felt alone. I thought about Nada and her Mate. I tried to imagine what it would feel like to know, even if I couldn't be with someone in person, they were somewhere out there caring about me and loving me. I needed a boyfriend. I rushed home to write down the rest of my plan to get one. First, I would look for someone I thought I wanted to be my boyfriend; then, when I'd decided, I would smile and say hello three times before I spoke to him. I would be subtle but persistent; there enough so he'd notice but not so much he would think I was stalking him. Then at the right time, I would offer to help him with his school work (or pretend I needed help with mine) and hopefully the rest would flow naturally.

Monday, August 26, 1991, was the first day of tenth grade. I was not the same person I was the last time I was in school; everything was different. I didn't have many first days of school left at that building. Next year, I would be a junior, then a senior, and then I would be in college. After that, I would never really be home again. Many times, I didn't feel like I was actually home then; I felt more like a transient, just passing through on my way to where I was really going. But where was I really going? I started with homeroom. I greeted all of the same faces that had been in my classes the past ten years.

"Ami." Krissa waved from a table in the back of the room. She tapped the top of the white plastic in the space next to her. "Sit here."

The metal chair scraped against the linoleum floor and I sat. The top of the table was marred with black; I tried to sweep the marks away with my hand but they were branded into the plastic, showing the use of the last three years since the school district decided to phase out lone-standing desks and fade in more flexible plastic garage-sale tables.

"How was your summer?" Krissa was cheerful, apparently not remembering the hell I went through toward the end of the school year. She had called me twice but I didn't want to talk, so I didn't answer and I didn't call her back. It hadn't seemed fair she could be living out her life happy and carefree while I was being forced to attempt to live life without Emily. It felt like that a little as I listened to Krissa talk about her summer; the vacation she went on with her family to Lake Tahoe and the afternoons she spent lounging at the city swimming pool. I felt somewhat betrayed by her oblivion to the fact I spent those same afternoons home alone trying to hold on to my sanity, but I had made an important decision about my life. So to honor the promise I made to myself, I smiled, listened, and nodded occasionally to present the impression I was interested.

"My mom said I can have a few friends over on Saturday night for a back-to-school get together; do you want to come?"

"Sure." My new plan for life seemed to be working. The last spot on our six-foot table was still empty when the tardy bell rang. I began to push the empty chair away to make more elbow room for Krissa when I looked up to see an unfamiliar face approaching. It was tan with brown eyes and short, straight brown hair which stood out from the disgusting short on top, long and curly in the back mullets that seemed to be the fad among the other boys at school. I frantically tried to remember the boyfriend-getting plan I had devised over the weekend and whispered, "Hi," as the boy sat down next to me. He smiled as he pulled his chair in closer to the table. I noticed he looked somewhat uncomfortable scrunched up against the table legs; then I looked over at Krissa and realized why. I scooted my chair back to the middle of the table. I said, "Sorry," to the grey specks in the plastic and didn't turn my head for the rest of homeroom to see if the new boy noticed my hands shaking as I tried to write notes about this year's rules and procedures.

Jodie Toohey

CHAPTER TWELVE

A little over a week later, I received a letter from Nada dated the exact day school started.

*   *   *   *   *

26 August 1991

Dear Ami,

Tata has been in Italy for a month. He finally came home to visit for the weekend last Friday. Maja and I rode our bikes all morning. Though the air was cloudy, we were filled with sunshine at thought of our family being together again. We struggled to propel our bicycles up steep hill toward our house. Our legs strained to rotate pedals. It was time for lunch and I was hungry. My stomach growled loudly and I giggled. I concentrated on pushing the pedals, my head down. When Maja stopped giggling with me and didn't ask what was so funny, I looked up thinking maybe she fell behind or raced ahead. But she was right there only a few feet in front of me, standing still and silent. I followed her eyes up the hill where a group of girls gathered in street. Some of them I recognized as my friends from school. I jumped off my bicycle and walked it up the hill to get a closer look. Maja followed. When I got closer, I saw Milana, a girl from my block who was a Serb like me. She was crying as girls surrounding her taunted her. They called her a dirty Serb and told her to go back to where she belongs. They said to go back to Serbia. Milana tried to tell them she'd never been to Serbia and her parents had never been to Serbia but they said they didn't care. They told her all Serbs need to go back to Serbia.

A pressure built in my chest. I didn't know what to do. I wanted to tell them to stop it, but I was afraid if I did, they would do the same thing to me even though some of them are my friends. It is complicated. They know I am a Serb but for some reason they are still my friends. They told me I don't act like a Serb. But how does a Serb act? I knew nothing other than pure luck of why Milana attracted ridicule for being Serb while my sister and I did not.

Milana's eyes met mine a moment before I turned and hurried with my bike to my house. As I worked with Maja to clean the house this afternoon, I noticed the clouds more than I had earlier in the day. It was not fair that Milana would be taunted and I would not. But it also was not fair that I was Serb and they were not. It was not fair we had to live alone while Tata worked in Italy.

The excitement bubbling in me at the thought of seeing Tata again, melted away. Mama came home and quickly changed clothes. She placed ingredients for our Gulas: beef, salt, pepper, paprika, bay leaf, and potatoes for boiling and serving under the Gulas onto counters. She flipped through the mail waiting in a stack on the kitchen table. Maja and I chatted with her about what time Tata would be home and how we would spend his weekend visit. She loosened the envelopes' flaps, examined contents, and then filed the bills and threw the advertisements in trash. Luckily there were no threat letters today.

We cooked supper as we waited for Tata. The clock did not seem to move. When the cuckoo announced seven o'clock and Tata was still not there, we worried. What if something happened to him? What if he crashed? My stomach was in knots and I feared I would be sick. But Mama, Maja, and I didn't mention it. We just continued to chat aimlessly about nothing in particular. Supper was ready. We kept the burners low and covered pans with lids to keep food warm. Finally, at seven twenty-three, the door flew open and Tata entered. Maja and I looked at each other. We whispered in unison, "He's home." We ran to him but he held out his hands to block our hugs.

"Hold it. Hold it," he said. "I couldn't wait to get home so I didn't shower. I just jumped in the car and started driving." Our homecoming celebration would have to wait. Mama followed Tata into bathroom. Maja and I sat back down at kitchen table to wait. A few minutes later, Tata emerged from bathroom with a cloud of steam closely behind.

"All right; where are those hugs?" We rushed to Tata. Maja hugged one side and I hugged other. At least for now we knew our world would be safe and happy.

The next morning, while Tata and Mama discussed house, bills, and mail, Maja and I went outside to play. We saw a group of our friends huddled in front of Milana's house and went to see what was happening. They told us Milana and her family had left. The family was there night before, but in morning, they were gone. I wondered if Milana's family had received same letters we had.

So I am still here in "war torn Yugoslavia" as they say on television. There is no fighting in Rijeka. We go on with our everyday lives like everything is normal. Except Tata is in Italy most of the time and more and more Serbs here leave in the middle of the night. I do not sleep much at night because I am afraid someone will come into kill us. I wonder why we stay but I guess we have nowhere else to go. We cannot go to my grandparents' house. They live by a tiny village called Kostajnica in Bosnia. A few weeks ago there was fighting in a village on River Una called Kozibrod as well as in Struga and Kuljani which are close to my grandparents' village. My grandparents are safe because they live on a farm away from the villages, but I hope they stay safe and the fighting does not get out into country. There has been a lot of fighting by Knin, in Banija, in eastern Slavonia by Osijek and Vukovar, and in Pakrac in western Slavonia. I do not know if you have a map of Yugoslavia so I will try to explain it to you. Knin is way down the coast of Croatia far away from my house and my grandparents' house. Kostajnica is close to my grandparents' house near the part of Croatia that bends. Slavonia is an area of Croatia which is inland between Bosnia to south, Hungary in the north, and Slovenia to west. It seems there has been fighting all over Croatia but not here yet. Mama is still working. Maja and I ride bikes all day. On television, they just show Serbs killing Croats but we hear people talking about Croats killing Serbs also.

Are you glad to be back home from your father's house? How is school? Our school will start back up in middle of September so I have a few weeks left. I am not anxious to go back to school. There is too much homework and studying. Please write me back when you can.

Your friend,
Nada

$$* \quad * \quad * \quad * \quad *$$

September 4, 1991

Dear Nada,

Thank you for your letter. I'm sorry the war is still going in your country, but I am glad the fighting is staying away from your town. I decided to try an experiment. I am going to concentrate on leaving my past behind and just having fun. The only time I will be serious is with my schoolwork because I need good grades to get into college and really on with my life. You are the only one I can share this revelation with because you are the only one who knows I've been somewhere else.

I am grateful my hell is only in my head and I have the ability to control and change it. You have no control over your hell and are at the mercy of what other people and your parents decide to do. Or not to do.

YES, there is a new cute boy in school and I've put my plan into action. His name is Andersen Simpson. He is from the state of California. I met him the first day of school when he walked into my homeroom class and sat down next to me. I liked him right away but was so nervous I couldn't even look at him that day. But, over the next few days, I gave myself pep talks and managed to smile at him and say, "Hello," to him whenever I saw him. And guess what? It worked! He smiled back at me more than he smiles at the guy-a-week girls who tried to flirt with him – or at least I think so (unless it is just my imagination). Last Saturday, I went to a party at my friend Krissa's house. Andy was there and he came over right away to talk to me. Unfortunately, I didn't get much of what he said because I was so distracted looking into his milk chocolate eyes and I was embarrassed for him to find out I wasn't listening so I didn't ask any questions. I did learn his parents went on a peacekeeping mission to Central America so he is living with his aunt and uncle until he goes back to California in December so he can finish tenth grade on time, can be a junior next fall, and graduate the year after next with his friends. He is very nice but seems so serious. He is not like the other boys in my class. He seems older somehow. And I could stare into his brown eyes forever. I wonder if this is love at first sight. Did you love Mate at first sight?

I almost didn't go to Krissa's party; I dreaded trying to talk to everyone and felt like just crawling into bed for the night. I didn't know Krissa invited Andy (that's what people are calling him). I bribed myself by telling myself if I was there an hour and not having any fun, I would come home. But then I got there, started talking to Andy, and actually enjoyed myself. I confessed to Krissa I think I like Andy so she said she will ask her parents if her boyfriend Craig, Andy, and I can come over next weekend to watch movies. I hope her parents agree. Since my birthday is on Tuesday, I will think of it like my birthday present.

Nada, do you wear makeup? I have never worn makeup before but I am thinking of asking my mom if I can start. If Krissa's parents let us come over next weekend, it will be like my first sort of date and I want to look pretty. I really want to get Andy to like me. He seems so nice. I never asked you: how did you and Mate come to be boyfriend and girlfriend?

I hope you enjoy the rest of your summer vacation and that your war is over soon!

You pen pal friend,
Ami

Jodie Toohey

CHAPTER THIRTEEN

"Hi, Ami." Krissa opened the door. "Andy and Craig are already downstairs." When I stepped off the bottom stair into Krissa's basement, Andy stood up from where he was sitting on a burlap-covered couch in oranges and yellows.

"Can I take your jacket?" Andy wore a dark blue shirt that buttoned down the front with tan pants.

"Sure." I took off my jacket, handed it to Andy, and he hung it on a hook on the wall near the bottom of the stairs.

Andy sat down on the end of the couch. "Do you want to sit down?" he asked. I sat on the edge of the middle cushion with my hands sandwiched between my knees.

"My mom said she would order us pizza," Krissa said. "What kind do you like?"

"Anything is fine," I said. Andy said, "I like anchovies."

"Except anchovies," I said, scrunching up my nose. Andy laughed.

I looked into his eyes and smiled. My heart thumped in my chest.

"I guess I'm outnumbered," Andy said. Krissa's and Craig's noses were scrunched as well. While Krissa went to order the pizza, Andy asked me about my family, their names, ages, and my parents' jobs. Krissa came back and sat on the arm of Craig's recliner.

"So, Andy, where exactly are your parents in Central America?" Craig asked.

"Guatemala." Thankfully Krissa and Craig asked Andy all of the requisite questions about his house, living in California, the rest of his family, and what he liked to do at home, so all I had to do was listen and try to remember everything he said. When the pizza arrived, Craig and Krissa moved to sit on bar stools and eat at the bar in the basement, leaving Andy and me to eat alone, sitting on the couch using the coffee table to hold our pizza. We ate in silence. When I was done, I sat back onto the couch. Andy did the same. Krissa and Craig were deep in a whispered conversation.

"So you have a mom, a dad, a brother, and a sister. You like to listen to music and read. What else do you like to do?" Andy pulled his leg up onto the couch and faced me more squarely.

"That pretty much covers it."

"That's it? What did you do all summer?"

"Just listened to music, read, and I walked a lot."

"Where did you walk?"

"Just around town mostly. I walked to the pier into the river by the library."

"Do you have any other family close by? Grandparents, aunts, uncles?"

"My grandparents live about forty-five minutes away. My Aunt Shari and Uncle Matt live close by, but we don't see them as much as we did before."

"Do you have any cousins?"

"Yeah, I…"

"Are they your age?"

"Younger, but…"

"What are their names?"

"Her name was Emily; she was a year old."

"I bet she is cute. Maybe I can meet her sometime?"

I felt a knot begin to form in my throat. "Emily died last March."

"I am so sorry." Andy smacked his forehead with the palm of his hand. "Here I am going on and on. I'm such an idiot."

I looked up into his eyes and could tell he felt really bad. "That's okay."

"I guess I'm a little nervous. I'm sorry." I held my breath to keep from crying and just shook my head. Andy took my hand in his. "Maybe you can tell me more about it sometime?"

"Maybe," I said.

Krissa swung around on her barstool. "What kind of party is this?" She slapped her hand onto the top of the bar and jumped down. "Should we play a game or watch a movie?"

We agreed on Trivial Pursuit. Andy and I played on a team and easily won the game. My heart fluttered every time Andy whispered what he thought the answer should be into my ear. Krissa put the game away and I sat back on the couch next to Andy. My right side was pressed next to his entire left side. I heard Andy talking, but I couldn't make out the words through my heart pounding in my ears.

"Ami, your mom is here for you," Krissa's mother yelled down the basement stairs.

"I'll be right there." The neon-bordered clock on the wall said 10:00. *Of course my mother is right on time, as usual*, I thought.

95

I stood up from the couch and faced Andy. He rose quickly and knocked me over.

"Whoa!" he said, grabbing my upper arms. "Sorry."

"That's okay." I looked up into his eyes and waited. Andy leaned toward me then stepped to the side.

"I'll get your jacket." He held it out to me and I tried to thrust my arms smoothly into the dangling sleeves.

"I'd better go," I said.

"I had fun," said Andy.

I shook my head in agreement. "Me, too." Then my breath stuck in my throat and I couldn't turn around. I stood there frozen for what felt like an eternity. Andy smiled at me.

Finally, Krissa said, "I'll call you tomorrow." I turned around, ran up the stairs, and out the front door.

"Don't you have something to say to Krissa's mom?"

I stepped back into the house. "Sorry. Thank you for having me."

"Well, thank you for coming, Ami; it was so nice to see you again."

I waved and went to sit in the car. My mom and Krissa's mom talked for a few more minutes.

"Did you have a nice time?" my mom asked. "What did you do?"

"Just had pizza and played Trivial Pursuit."

"Was it fun?"

My mom told me about her night; she and Aunt Shari watched *Dances with Wolves* on the VCR, and ate popcorn and fudge. When we were almost home she said, "I should've came in to meet your new friend. What was his name?"

"Andy."

"Maybe he can come over to our house some time."

The house of doom? I thought, but just said, "Okay."

I spent the next week writing about every detail of my night in a letter I'd send to Nada after I received her next letter. It finally arrived on the 16th.

*   *   *   *   *

10 September 1991

Dear Ami,

I got your letter in the mail today. Happy Birthday!

We have secrets in our house now. I need to tell someone. Tata's cousin, Stevo, came to live with us last week with his wife, Marija. Stevo is a Serb from Mostar in Bosnia and Marija is Roman Catholic. Mostar is in southern Bosnia about twenty or thirty miles from border with Croatia's southernmost tip, the Dalmatian coast. Marija is pregnant so they came to live with us so Stevo wouldn't be drafted. Marija can go out because she is Roman Catholic but nobody can know Stevo is here. He has to hide in our house. If he was to go out and someone would ask for his identification, he could be taken away or killed. We have to keep our curtains closed so neighbors won't see him inside of our house. We like Marija and do not care she is not Catholic Orthodox. Marija does not care that we are not Roman Catholic. It is unfair our neighbors should care and hate us. They are not in our family and they are not in our house. What should it matter to them who is living with us? It makes me so angry sometimes but not so angry I want to hurt them. Even if they are angry, I don't understand how they could be so angry they would do something to take Stevo away from his wife and child.

Perhaps our neighbors only believe what they hear on

television. Please do not believe everything you hear on television, especially if your news reports are like news reports here. The only thing they talk about is how Serbs are killing Croats. But Croats are killing Serbs, too. The news talks about Serb soldiers killing people, burning them, and raping women but they don't tell about Croatian army burning down churches with Serbs locked inside. We hear these stories. They don't care if Serb is against them or a soldier. They put any Serbs they can find, young and old, into the church, lock the doors, and burn it down.

Now, in addition to not being able to look at the mail until after our parents look through it, we are also not allowed to answer telephone. We are beginning to get threatening telephone calls along with the letters. I can tell when it is one of those calls because Mama's face turns white, she hangs up abruptly, and smiles like someone dialed a wrong number. I know these are people calling to tell us to leave our home or be killed because my few Catholic Orthodox friends have told me they received same calls. I considered telling Mama and Tata I know about the threats but they seem comforted by believing Maja and I do not know what is happening. They worry about so much already. I do not want them to have to worry about my feelings along with everything else. I am sure you understand. I will be okay as long as I have a good friend like you to share my secrets.

Even though I felt bad for Stevo and Marija to have to run away from their home, I am happy they are staying with us. Mama, Maja, and I are going to help them get ready for their baby. It is due in February. They didn't have anything for the baby when they left Bosnia and wouldn't have had space in their car to bring it with them if they had. As soon as Mama returned from work after they arrived in the middle of the afternoon, she dug out her old sewing patterns from when Maja and I were babies. While Stevo set up a bed and their space in the basement, we girls picked patterns to use to make Stevo and Marija baby clothes. We are planning to go to fabric store on Saturday to get the cloth. Mama says Maja and I can help pin the tissue patterns to fabric, trace them with a wheel and carbon paper, and then cut out the pieces for her and Marija to sew. It will be fun to have something else to do besides go to school, ride bikes, and try not to watch the news.

I am anxious for school to start on Monday so I can see my friends and Mate. I miss Mate. He has not come to visit me much since his parents forbid him from spending time with me. He told me his parents still like me and my family. The problem is they are afraid if their Croat neighbors see them associating with a Serb, they will turn against them. At school, I think I can forget about the war. Though we pretend it isn't, the war is always with me. Even as I ride my bike and pretend to be carefree, my breath is always tense wondering if someone will jump from the bushes to taunt me like they did to Milana. At home, even when we have been happily pinning patterns to fabric and sewing to make baby clothes, guessing about if the baby will look more like Stevo or Marija, it is heavy over us. Even when the television and radio are turned off. Every noise makes an invisible jump in our skins because we fear they are coming to get us. We freeze when phone rings and remain still without so much as taking a breath until we can tell from Mama's voice it is not another threat call.

This evening, we cleaned the kitchen after dinner and started our baby clothes project like we had yesterday. Stevo sat at kitchen table finishing his tea and thinking. He said he was thinking about what he will do and where they can go when the baby is born. He will need a job to take care of it and hopes the war will be over by then because he could not make much money hiding out in our house. Mama and Tata told him not to worry. They said Stevo, Marija, and the baby could stay and they would provide for them as long as necessary. But Stevo said it gave him something to occupy his mind all during the long hours at home.

Maja had just made sure the edges of the folded green fabric lined up precisely and I was inserting a straight pin to secure the pajama leg pattern piece to it when we heard a knock at door. Our curtains were open a few inches to let in some fresh late summer air so Stevo could have seen down to front door, but he was so deep in thought, he didn't. I flinched and stuck my left index finger with needle. A dot of blood began to grow but I didn't wipe it away. I just stared at it. I was frozen, hoping it would not drip onto fabric.

"Stevo," Marija hissed. Stevo didn't hear her. "Stevo!"

Stevo shuttered back to present and looked at Marija.

"Someone's at the door," Marija whispered.

As casually as he could, Stevo pushed the chair under table and left for the basement.

"Just a minute." I could tell Mama was feigning cheer. She acted like she had fresh baked chocolate chip cookies she had to remove from the oven before answering. She smoothed her hair and opened the door just enough she could see who had knocked.

"Yes?"

The narrow door opening muffled the visitor but I heard, "My name is," and immediately stuck the tip of my finger in my mouth to remove the blood. I took a deep breath. It hurt in middle of my back because I had been so tense and still trying to keep blood from ruining the baby's new pajamas. I figured someone coming to kill us or drive us from our home wouldn't announce his name, so I relaxed.

Mama opened the door wider, "Come in."

The visitor was a Jehovah's Witness. Later, I heard Mama whisper to Marija she let him in house so in case he was a spy, he would see we have nothing to hide. Stevo now says he will not leave the basement. He says after helping to cook dinner, Marija can bring him a plate of food for him to eat down there.

Did you get to see Andy last weekend? What did you do for your birthday? I am happy you seem happier. I hope your plan is working and you are getting closer to making Andy your boyfriend.

Your friend,
Nada

Jodie Toohey

CHAPTER FOURTEEN

September 17, 1991

Dear Nada,

I remember when my aunt was pregnant with Emily. It was so exciting and so much fun to get ready for it to be born. Is the baby kicking yet? It feels funny to put your hand on the outside of the belly and feel the baby kicking your hand. If Stevo and Marija still need to stay at your house when the baby is born, you will love holding it. My advice? Make sure you take advantage of every moment because in a moment, the baby could be gone, just like Emily.

My plan for making Andy my boyfriend is progressing. Two weekends ago, we had a double date with Krissa and her boyfriend. We talked and sat side by side on the couch while we played Trivial Pursuit. (It is a game. Do you have it there?) Last Saturday at 1:00 p.m., Andy came over to my house and we went for a walk to the park. About halfway there, Andy's hand kept bumping mine as we were walking on the sidewalk. I thought, *I am so clumsy*, then, on one bump, he grabbed my hand. My heart was beating so fast I thought my voice must have been shaking but Andy didn't seem to notice. At the park, we sat on a bench by the playground and watched the little kids play. That made me a little sad because I started to think about Emily. She would have been two next month and would be the age of a lot of the little kids climbing up the playground stairs and giggling while they slid down the slides. Then, something great happened. We sat there quiet watching the kids and then all of a sudden Andy took my left hand in both of his.

Andy said, "Are you okay, Ami?"

"Yes." I looked at him and smiled.

"What are you thinking?"

"Just watching the kids," I said.

Andy squeezed my hand in his, "I want to talk to you about something." For a second, I was worried, but his eyes were so warm I knew he wasn't going to say anything to hurt me.

"Okay."

"I was wondering if you would be my date for the homecoming dance."

I said, "Yes," of course. And I almost had my first kiss – I think. Andy held my hand all the way home. We didn't talk much. I was too busy enjoying my hand in his.

When we got to my house, he took both of my hands and faced me. He said, "Thank you for walking with me." He started to lean toward me but my heart was beating so hard I thought I was going to vomit so I turned my head away.

The homecoming dance is a little over one month away on October 19th and I can't wait. My mom called my dad; he said he would pay for a new dress, so my mom and I are going to go shopping one Saturday soon to find one. I'm thinking I will get a pink or a blue one. I will send you a picture!

I hope everything is okay with you. How is school? Please write me back when you can.

Your friend,
Ami

*   *   *   *   *

25 September 1991

Dear Ami,

Last Monday, 16 September, was my first day of the grade eight. Maja and I said goodbye to Stevo and Marija, put our backpacks on, closed the door, and started walking toward school. We wore our best jeans and nicest shirts. We agreed it would be fun to see our friends but a pain to do homework and study again, but when we got almost to school, my mood changed. I couldn't explain to myself why. It was just suddenly apparent our feelings the new school year would be especially good were misguided. Our friends smiled and waved to us as they always did but something felt different. I did not know how or why.

When bell rang, Maja went to her first class. My classmates and I filed into ours. A pile of cream colored folders were stacked on top of the teacher's desk. He stood in front of the rows of desks. He told us to line up single file to side of desk. He fanned the folders out, asked the first student in line her name, and then plucked the folder with her name typed on the tab, and opened the cover. Based on some information unknown to me in the folder, Mr. Jovanović assigned her a desk. He had a sloppy drawn grid where he wrote her name in the square corresponding to desk he'd just assigned in the front right corner. I was next in line. Mr. Jovanović took my name, pointed me to a desk in the back row, wrote my name in the corresponding box in his grid, and then opened my folder to confirm what he apparently already knew. One by one, Mr. Jovanović assigned desks to each person in line. When all of the desks in front three rows were filled, he asked remaining kids in line their names and looked in their folders without assigning them a desk. He rearranged the desks so only four remained in the furthest back row. When everyone had taken their seats, I noticed the other three students in the class I knew to be Catholic Orthodox were the only students left in back row.

Everything is different now. Everyone, even people who were not my friends, were always nice and friendly. Now they whisper and stare. Who was Serb or Croat and who was Catholic Orthodox or Roman Catholic used to not matter, but now it seems it is all that matters. In all of my classes, I sit in the back row with just my Catholic Orthodox classmates. My teachers are nice to me even though they put me in back row. Maybe they know I earn A's and that is saving me. In language class, we spent first half writing an essay about our favorite author or book. We read while the teacher graded our essays. He returned them during the last ten minutes of class. My essay had one or two red marks more than most all of students sitting in the rows in front of me but much less than the students in my own back row.

The war is getting worse. Stevo and Marija are still living with us but Stevo is living entirely in our basement. There have been rumors of military police searching houses to find men who ignored their calls to fight so Stevo has been talking about trying to escape away from Yugoslavia. But they do not have anywhere to go and Marija does not want to go where she doesn't know anyone while she is pregnant. For the same reason, Tata has not been home for a visit in weeks. He is in Italy legally so he cannot be forced to come back but he is afraid if he does come back, the army will capture him and drag him off to fight. I saw on news a peace conference was held in The Hague in the Netherlands. What a joke that is! Less than a week after the so-called peace conference, thirteen Serb prisoners were killed on a bridge between Korana and Karlovac which is in Croatia's narrowest point that is not bordered by water, a little over halfway from Rijeka to Zagreb. The news said the JNA (Yugoslav Army) is trying to divide Croatia at this same point in order to defeat Croat army. I do not care if we are in Yugoslavia or Croatia. I just want this war to end so I can go visit my grandparents.

We have had two practice drills so we know what to do in case bombing starts in Rijeka. An alarm sounds and we walk one behind each other to a bomb shelter. It is dark and small so I hope we never have to use it for real.

Please write back soon!

Your friend,
Nada

CHAPTER FIFTEEN

The weeks leading up to the dance ticked by. I tried to keep busy by spending time with Andy or Krissa, and living as normal of a teenager life as I could. Mom insisted that Aunt Shari come with us to buy my dress. She said it would do Aunt Shari good to get out of the house. She couldn't have been more wrong. At first, Aunt Shari was cheerful, helping me pick out dresses to try on. As I tried on each one, Aunt Shari's smile faded. Mom went out to find a version of a pink dress in the correct size rather than the wrong one we brought in. I looked in the mirror wearing the same dress in the seventh shade of blue. I saw Aunt Shari behind me in the mirror.

"You look beautiful," she said, but I could see tears glossed over her eyes. She tried to smile through it, but couldn't. I turned to look at her.

"I'm sorry, Ami," she said, and buried her head in her hands. I didn't know what to do.

"Mom!" I called into the store.

"What is it?" she said. She tossed an armload of dresses down on a chair in the corner. I pointed toward Aunt Shari.

"I'm sorry," Aunt Shari said again. "I guess I'm just not ready yet."

"That's okay. Ami and I can come back tomorrow. Isn't that right?"

"Sure. Let's go home," I said.

When I got home, Grandma, who was babysitting Forti and Prio, said Krissa called. She had an extra babysitting job and asked if I wanted it. I should've remembered the dress store with Aunt Shari and said, "No," but I didn't. The Masterson's kids were Forti and Prio's ages so I thought it would be different enough. It wasn't.

The Masterson's saying goodbye reminded me of how Emily would hug and kiss each of her parents twice before they left. Scooping Carry's and Jimmy's ice cream for their bed time snack reminded me of feeding Cheerios to Emily.

I tucked Carry and then Jimmy into bed. I turned on the TV. Soon I heard giggling behind the wall. I peeked around the corner and saw them crouched down, their mouths tucked into the tops of their pajamas, giggling. I started to cry.

They were stunned. Their hands dropped to their sides and they stared at me.

"We're sorry," Jimmy said.

"Please don't tell Mommy and Daddy," Carry said.

I waved them to the living room and patted the couch cushions. They climbed up as my tears came harder. I tried to wipe them away and compose myself so I could talk.

Carry said, "We were just trying to have fun. We didn't mean to be naughty."

"We not naughty," Jimmy echoed.

"No, you weren't naughty. It is just that you reminded me of something that makes me very sad."

I turned the TV to the Disney Channel and let them stay up. When they fell asleep, I allowed the tears to come back, crying as quietly as I could.

*   *   *   *   *

October 20, 1991

Dear Nada,

How are you? The bomb shelter drills sound spooky. I remember when I was littler we would have air-raid-siren drills. We have sirens that go off when we have a severe thunderstorm or tornado and during the air-raid drills, they would make a different swooping sound. All of the kids in class had to take a book, crouch under their desks, and put the books over their heads. The tornado drills were basically the same but we had to crouch and put the books over our heads in the hallways. We haven't had the air-raid-siren drills for a few years; I guess since Gorbechev "tore down that wall," the school doesn't think we need them anymore. With what is happening in your country, I'm not so sure I'd be as trusting as I was back then.

It is six o'clock on Sunday morning here and I can't sleep. I keep thinking about the dance last night. And Andy. I cannot believe a boy like Andy actually likes me and wants to spend time with me. Maybe guardian angels are real. Maybe Emily is my guardian angel and has brought me Andy. I will tell you about it here in detail. We only live about a half mile from my school so Andy and I walked there. He picked me up at 6:30; the sun had just set so the sky was mostly dark blue with a sliver of orange on the west horizon, like candlelight. He came in the house, I gave him his boutonniere flower, and my mom pinned it to his sweater (dark green with tan pants – very handsome).

He said, "Was I supposed to get you a flower?"

I didn't know what to say but my mom saved me. "Sometimes boys will get girls a wrist corsage for dances but it's not required," she said.

"I didn't know." Andy looked into my eyes. "I'm sorry." The poor boy looked devastated.

"It's okay," I said. "It doesn't matter." My mom took our picture in front of the staircase while Forti and Prio made kissing noises in the kitchen. They had been doing it all day so my mom told them they had to go into the kitchen and wait when Andy picked me up, but now that Andy was there, they knew she wouldn't yell at them.

Andy held my hand all the way to the dance. We were mostly quiet. I wanted to ask him about living in California; whether it was as warm all year as they say it is, whether he surfs, or whether he has a palm tree in his backyard. I wanted to ask about his parents, about their mission work, his friends, and whether he had any cousins or aunts or uncles. But I didn't. I really wanted to and I would finally decide what I was going to say in my head, but then I couldn't make my mouth move to speak. Once I made a squeaking sound. He looked at me but I coughed. Then we got to the dance and it was too late.

The gym at school was decorated with shades of red, yellow-orange, and brown leaves; they had paper trees mounted on the wall with the limbs arched over the dance floor with the leaves hanging down. I could hardly imagine playing basketball in gym class in the same space just the day before. We had our picture taken in front of a giant poster that looked like a lane lined with trees with yellow leaves.

A DJ played cassettes and CDs. I danced the fast dances with Krissa and some other girls from school while the boys watched from the tables set up on both sides of the dance floor. After every two or three fast songs, they played slow songs and all the boys would come out to the dance floor to find their dates or others girls to ask to dance. I clasped my hands behind Andy's neck, he put his hands on each side of my hips, and we turned around in circles. The first time, my heart was beating so fast I had trouble breathing, but then I got more comfortable. By the third dance, I rested my cheek on Andy's shoulder and closed my eyes. I felt like I was on a merry-go-round. About halfway through the dance, Krissa, Craig, another friend of Krissa's, her date, Andy, and I took a break from dancing to drink some punch.

Out of nowhere, Andy said, "I want to show you something."

Andy took my cup of punch from my hand and set it down on the table. He laced his fingers through mine and led me across the dance floor behind where the DJ was set up. On a wall behind the DJ were stapled artificial flowers my mom later told me were mums with the names of everyone who was at the dance written on a piece of paper and attached to the flowers. Andy picked the flower with our names by it from the wall and put it in my hand. A slow song started to play. He didn't say anything but just gently pulled me to the dance floor and we started dancing. This time, he put his hands all the way around my waist. I held onto the flower for the rest of the night and I put it in my keepsake box when I got home so I have it forever. I have mementos of everything important to me in my keepsake box, including the pajamas Emily was wearing the last time I saw her alive and the teddy bear I made her in sewing class last year that Aunt Shari gave me after Emily died. Anyway, back to my story. This is a happy story so I don't want to make myself sad by thinking about Emily.

So except when I had to use the restroom or put on my jacket when we left, the flower stayed in my one hand and my other hand stayed in Andy's hand. After what seemed like five minutes had passed, it was nine o'clock already and the dance was over. We walked back to my house much slower than we had walked to the dance and Andy talked more. He told me about his friends in California; I tried to commit their names to memory. I missed a couple of the names and wanted to ask him, but again, I couldn't. We walked up toward the front step of my house; Andy stopped just beyond the reach of the porch light. He faced me and stared straight into my eyes. I thought he was going to kiss me, but he kicked the pebbles on the sidewalk and then he looked back up at me without fully lifting his head. I looked back at him and thought, *Kiss me! Kiss me!* Finally, he leaned down and kissed me. I know Mate has kissed you so you know how it feels, but I want to write down every detail so I can remember it always. His top lip went between my lips and my bottom lip between his; he kind of gently sucked my bottom lip in and I did the same with his. We stayed like this for about one second then moved apart a fraction of an inch and did it again. Then I did the craziest thing – I started to cry!

"Was it that bad?"

"No." I wiped tears from my eyes. "I don't know what's the matter with me. No one has ever kissed me like that before. I'm sorry."

"It's okay," he said, and then he hugged me really tight. He walked me to my front door and kissed me quickly one more time before leaving. When he got to the sidewalk by the road, he turned around and waved to me.

I want to remember every moment of last night. I couldn't sleep because I kept replaying it in my head. Luckily, I am making a copy of what I am writing in this letter so I have it forever.

I needed the dance last night. A week ago on October 12th, Emily would have turned two years old. My mom, Forti, and Prio spent the day at Aunt Shari's house. Uncle Matt went out with his friends to drink beer and watch college football on TV. My mom wanted me to go because she said it would help Aunt Shari to be around people who loved Emily, but I talked her into letting me stay at home. I don't like to see Aunt Shari. I still love her, but when I see her, I think Emily should be there with her but she isn't, and it just reminds me she's gone. Maybe that's why Uncle Matt goes out so much. I bought a bottle of soda at the convenience store and then sat on the pier while I drank it and wrote a letter to Emily. I dried out the bottle as much as I could after it was empty, rolled up the letter, and stuck it inside. I capped the bottle and threw it into the river. I cried as I watched it wash away. Then I came back home and, except for when I saw Andy, I felt sad all week. Now I am starting to feel sad again so I will end this letter and think about the dance more.

I hope everything is okay where you are. Write back soon!

Your friend,
Ami

*   *   *   *   *

I wrote to Nada what I wanted to remember and didn't mention what I wanted to forget. When I got in the door after the dance that night, the lights were on but the house was silent.

"Mom?" I said. Nothing. I yelled, "Mom!?" My stomach turned sick.

"I'm up here, Ami." It sounded like my mom but the voice was different; muffled. I went upstairs.

"Mom? Where are you?"

"In my bedroom." The door was open a few inches and orange light streamed into the dark hallway. I pushed it open.

"How was the dance?" She went into her bathroom, turning her robed back to me. She came back out wiping her face with a wet washcloth. "Is it after nine already?"

I pointed to the red digits on her alarm clock. "It's almost 9:30."

"I was just washing my face. I guess I lost track of time." Her eyes were red and puffy around the outside. "So how was the dance? Did you have a good time?"

"Yeah." Then I remembered the quiet and before ten on Saturday night. I gasped slightly. "Are Forti and Prior in bed already?"

"No. Your dad called and asked if they could come spend the night. I hope that's okay. I didn't think you would mind them going without you. Your dad said he could take you out for lunch tomorrow if you felt left out."

"It's okay. I'm fine."

My mom sat down on the edge of her bed and patted the space next to her. I sat down. She rubbed my back. "Tell me about the dance."

I described the decorations and showed her the flower Andy picked off the wall for me.

"How sweet. I hope you didn't make him feel too bad about forgetting to get you a flower."

"No. I told him again it was okay and he gave me this one so he made up for it." Tears began to collect again so I quickly changed the subject, "What did you do tonight?"

She told me she went to visit Aunt Shari for a little while. "Uncle Matt went out with his friends and Aunt Shari was having a bad night so I took a pizza and a bottle of wine over to share with her." I was going to confront my mom about her crying, but then her tears suddenly made sense. She lost a niece when Emily died but she had to be strong for her sister who lost a daughter. I decided to leave her to her tears and hugged her.

"I'm tired. I think I'm going to go to bed."

"Ami?" I turned in the doorway and looked back. She wiped her eye with the wash cloth. "I love you."

117

"I love you, too, Mom. Goodnight."

A few minutes after I lay down in bed, I heard the TV turn on downstairs. I turned my attention to replaying my night.

CHAPTER SIXTEEN

28 October 1991

Dear Ami,

Your night with Andy at your dance sounds so magical and romantic. I am so happy your plan to get a boyfriend is working.

The war has still, thankfully, not moved into Rijeka but it is getting worse in the rest of Croatia. Some of the army has actually left this area to concentrate on other parts of Croatia. I lie awake at night waiting but, somehow, I have become used to it. My dad has not been home in weeks. Marija's belly is getting bigger and that makes me happy. Mostly, my life is still same: school, chores, and talking with Stevo and Marija about the baby. Nobody talks about religion or the war. Earlier in month a couple of dozen Serbs, just regular people, not army, were killed in Gospic which is southwest of Rijeka about 120 kilometers. In Zagreb, now Croatia's capital city, which is only a little farther away at 130 kilometers and northeast of Rijeka along the main highway, they killed a whole family of Serbs, including the twelve-year-old daughter. At night, sometimes I have nightmares they come into my house. They knock on door with their fists and pound upstairs to my bed. I try to plead with them, tell them I am only fourteen, my sister is only twelve, and Marija is going to have a baby but they just laugh. They do not care about age or anything else. All they care about is Maja and I are Serbs in "their" Croatia. Then I tell them Marija is not Serb but she is Roman Catholic. They say she is living with Serbs and married to a Serb so that does not matter either. Every time, just as I see the flash of red from the end of some of their guns reflecting off the knife blades of the others, I jump up in bed, sweat dripping into my eyes even though it is the end of October and not hot outside anymore.

Dubrovnik seems to be getting the worst of the attacks. The city is down on the Dalmatian coast where Croatia is narrowest. You can't even get to Dubrovnik only by land without passing right by Bosnia and Herzegovina so maybe that is why. It is cut off and they can get at it easily. I heard that shelling destroyed Dubrovnik's 500 year old arboretum. On television, they show bombed out Dubrovnik with people unable to go to their homes, living without water, electricity, or telephones.

Do you hear anything about this war on your television? At first it seemed like America was mad at Croatia for declaring its independence from Yugoslavia and was taking sides with Serbia to keep the country together. Now it seems like America is blaming the Serbs for the war. How do you feel about it? Does it even matter to you? I feel like we all got along before, Serbs, Croats, Muslims, and everyone else and I don't understand why it matters now. My friends are my friends.

Tonight when I am trying to go to sleep I will think about you and Andy. I will imagine myself at your dance with you, Andy, and Mate, and maybe I won't have any nightmares.

Please write back.

Your friend,
Nada

*　　*　　*　　*　　*

On Halloween, I wanted to hide. I had already told Andy I planned to block out the world during trick-or-treat by screaming music through my headphones. Emily would've been two years old and the perfect age to trick-or-treat; old enough to understand the fun of getting candy, but young enough to be adorable and excited. Last year, Emily had started to roar; out of nowhere she would yell "Raahr!" It could've been while watching TV or at the checkout lady at the grocery store. I suggested to Aunt Shari that Emily should be a lion next year for Halloween so Aunt Shari bought a lion costume with fake muscles and a stuffed tail on clearance to save. I couldn't stand to watch other little kids going door to door for their treats, so I didn't want to take Forti and Prio out. The thought of people bringing little kids to my door to ask for candy when my Emily was gone made me inexplicably angry. So when my mom asked me if I wanted to take Forti and Prio trick-or-treating or if I wanted to stay home and hand out candy, I told her I wanted to skip Halloween. She sighed but didn't say any more about it.

In the afternoon, Andy surprised me with a miniature

jack-o- lantern-shaped bucket full of candy. He held my hand and we walked around the block.

"I wish I would've been able to meet Emily," he said.

"Me, too. You would have loved each other."

"Tell me about her." He draped his arm over my shoulder. I turned toward him and it fell off.

"I can't. It's too hard," I said.

"Why don't you ever talk to me?"

"I talk to you," I said.

"No, you don't, not really. What are you thinking? What are you feeling?"

"I don't know." I held my breath to try to prevent myself from crying.

"I just want to talk to you about real things."

I clenched my fists and my jaw. "Why do we have to do this today?"

"We don't. I'm sorry." Andy folded his arms in front of his chest and we walked the rest of the block silent. I spent the night with my lights out, a pillow over my head with just the cord of my headphones connected to my stereo. When the doorbell stopped, I pulled the earphones out and went to sleep.

The next day, I called Andy and tried to explain. I had so much seriousness in my life that when I was with him I just wanted to be light, have fun, and laugh. He said maybe it was better that way so it would be easier when he went back home. I didn't ask him what he meant.

CHAPTER SEVENTEEN

November 6, 1991

Dear Nada,

I do not watch the news a lot but it does seem like they mention the bad things Serbs are doing there. Don't worry, it doesn't matter to me. I was baptized at a Lutheran church, but I can't remember the last time I even went to church, though it was probably Prio's baptism. Here, it doesn't matter what religion you are. I learned in government class we have a "separation clause" which basically says religion and government can have nothing official to do with each other and they have to separate. So people have friends with people of all different religions – Catholic, Protestant, Baptist, Buddhist, etc. and there are several churches that have the same religion – if you go to the same church, you do things with your friends at church and if you don't, you can visit their church or you can just get together outside of church. For people who go to church, it is mostly a few hours out of their Sunday mornings; for the rest of us, it's just something you say about yourself when people ask, like "What do you like on your pizza?" You are not going to shun someone or hate them because they like mushrooms on their pizza and you don't.

Things with Andy are going good. We had a little "issue" around Halloween, but that is all better now. I was having a bad day and he wanted to talk about serious things; we decided it's better to keep things light and fun. He will be going back to California in a little less than six weeks, so I want to spend the time making happy memories. Speaking of memories, last Saturday Andy and I watched the movie, *Kindergarten Cop*, which we rented. It was about a police officer who looks like a body builder and goes undercover as a kindergarten teacher to try to catch a drug dealer. At the end, Andy said he wants to make crazy memories before he goes back to California, so I have a surprise for him for after the last football game this Friday. I don't want to jinx it so I will write more about it after I do it, but I will say it involves the baseball dugout and a tealight candle.

I have some other news. We have something in common: one of my relatives is now living in our house. I suppose my relative is hiding from something, but not in the sense your relative is hiding from something. It is my Aunt Shari. She and my Uncle Matt are getting a divorce. Apparently, my Uncle Matt went out drinking with his friends again on Saturday night and he didn't come home until eight on Sunday morning. I don't blame my Aunt Shari for getting mad; when someone you are close to dies, you start to worry every time someone is late or is not where they said they would be. Have you ever experienced that? Anyway, when Uncle Matt finally came home, they got into a huge fight. Uncle Matt went to a friend's house and Aunt Shari came here. On Monday while I was at school, Mom and Aunt Shari went to talk to a divorce lawyer and then yesterday she and Uncle Matt put their house up for sale. She is going to stay with us until they sell the house and she can get an apartment of her own. The good news for me is another adult living in the house means less babysitting for me and since I don't have my license yet, another driver will be available, which hopefully will mean more time with Andy. I want to spend every minute I can with him until he leaves. The bad news is Aunt Shari took Forti's room, so now we have to sleep together in my room in my bed. I feel sorry for my Aunt Shari and I hugged her when she came over Sunday, but I've spent all the time when I'm not eating or using the bathroom in my bedroom. For one, since Forti is sleeping here, I get almost no time for myself so want to take advantage of it when I can and for two, there has been a lot of crying, which challenges my be-light, have-fun goals.

Have you felt the baby kick yet? Write back when you can.

Your friend,
Ami

*   *   *   *   *

23 November 1991

Dear Ami,

I have felt the baby kick. We have so much fun with it. Marija lies down on the couch then we push in her belly at different spots and the baby will kick back. We say it is going to be smart since it is already playing games.

We are in another "ceasefire," which means little. Maja and I joke when they mention another ceasefire on television and make bets as to how long this one will last. We have had to debate our bets on this latest ceasefire in whispers after we went to bed, though, because Mama heard us the time before. She said it was poor manners to make bets over people's lives. She said we could not do it again. Much of Dubrovnik has been destroyed. There are far fewer people left there. The ones who stayed are without electricity and have only a little bit of food to eat and water to drink. Four days ago, there was a big battle in Vukovar. Vukovar is in far eastern Croatia on border of the Vojvodina province in Serbia. Many people were killed. Yesterday, all of television stations were filled with an interview of Margaret Thatcher, who asked for Croatia and the other Yugoslavia republics who have declared independence, to be recognized. I am hopeful if Serbia gives up on trying to keep Croatia from becoming independent, the fighting will stop and we can go to see my grandparents. I miss them so much and am so hungry for my grandmother's cooking.

Winter is coming. It is getting colder. It is too cold to even go outside to ride bikes. We just go to school, study, do chores, and watch television. And play with Marija's belly. Mama, Maja, Stevo, Marija, and I are all trying to pick out a name. We have a list of boys' names and a list of girls' names taped to our refrigerator. Every time we walk by, we say names out loud then make a mark next to one we like the best that time. We try to say them all different ways: happy, excited, sad, stern. So far it is a tie.

I'm sorry to hear about your aunt and uncle getting divorced. Maybe losing Emily was too much for them. Maybe like your Aunt Shari reminding you Emily is gone and making you feel sad, so you like to avoid her, they remind each other. How was your "crazy memory" with Andy? Did it work? Was he surprised? I can't wait to hear about it. Write back soon!

Your friend,
Nada

CHAPTER EIGHTEEN

On November 15th, Andy and I went to the last football game of the year. When I met him at my front door with my large purse holding my supplies, he looked at me weird. I told him I had a surprise. Throughout the whole game, he kept trying to guess the surprise, get me to give him hints, and peek in my purse. But I wouldn't crack. I told him he had to wait and sat with my purse straps knotted through my arms. After the final buzzer of the game, he jumped up and said, "Is it time for the surprise?"

I relieved my arms of my purse straps, pushed them up my shoulder, and grabbed Andy's hand. I led him down the bleachers and outside of the football stadium; after we cut away from the direction the crowd exited and got beyond the parking lot lights, he whispered in my ear, "Where are we going?"

"You'll see." I pulled him ahead and looked over my shoulder. Once I was sure nobody saw us and couldn't see us, I gave Andy the blindfold I borrowed from Prio's pin-the-tail-on-the-donkey game. "Put this on."

Along the ground, I shined the light from the mini flashlight I had hid in my purse behind the football stadium, across the soccer fields to the baseball diamonds on the far edge of the school property. It was dark and spooky with the dugouts of the baseball diamond facing a row of trees with cornfields behind them. If it wasn't for Andy and then the flashlight, I would've been too scared to make it that far. I thought about asking Andy to take off the blindfold, but I didn't want to ruin the surprise. Halfway to the diamond, I heard a swoosh and sheets of rain poured down on us. I ran, pulling Andy behind me, trying not to fall or make him fall. When we reached the home team dugout, we were drenched and laughing.

"Can I take this off now?" Andy gasped for breath.

I sat him down on the two-by-four of unfinished wood that served as a bench. "Just a couple of more minutes. Let me get set up." I carefully unwrapped the paper towels from the wine glasses I borrowed from our kitchen cupboard.

I thought I was going to get caught when my mom noticed they were missing the night before. She called me down to the kitchen from my room.

"Ami, have you seen my wine glasses?" she asked. I shrugged my shoulders.

"Are you sure you didn't break one when you were doing dishes?

"Because it's okay if you did; you can tell me."

I started to feel nervous. "I didn't break anything. If I would've, I would've told you."

"Okay; I'm just asking."

"I haven't seen any wine glasses in the dirty dishes lately."

She said, "Aunt Shari must have them in Forti's room."

I made it and I didn't really lie. I didn't break anything and I hadn't seen the wine glasses in the dirty dishes.

In the dugout, I slowly turned the cap off the bottle of soda I'd bought; it hissed and I was afraid it was too shaken up from my running. I poured the soda into the glasses. I lit the tealight candle I'd taken from my mom's supply with the matches that luckily stayed dry in the middle of my purse. I had also brought a little radio already set to a station that played romantic music in the evenings, but it was in the outside pocket of my purse. When I turned it on, it crackled and then went silent, so I tucked it back in my purse and slid it under the bench. I stood so Andy could see the candle and an occasional stray raindrop fell on my forearm. "Okay, I'm ready."

Andy stood up and lifted the blindfold over his head. I extended one of the glasses of soda to him and he took it. "Here's to crazy memories," I said. Andy smiled. We tapped our glasses together and took a drink.

"Vintage cola," he said. "My favorite." Then he took my glass from my hand and put both of them down on the bench. He put his arms around my waist, pulled me close, and we started to dance in circles. I laid my head on his shoulder and we danced to our own music and that of the rain for the longest time. I didn't want to leave, but at the last possible second to make it home before my ten o'clock curfew, we packed up and jogged back to my house. Andy kissed me once. When I turned to walk toward my door to go in, he pulled me back by my arm, kissed me again longer, and hugged me really tight. I think he may have been starting to cry because right after that, he turned and walked quickly away. Maybe it was foreshadowing of what happened next.

*   *   *   *   *

December 9, 1991

Dear Nada,

I have another good news and bad news letter; mostly bad news. I will start with the good news. My crazy memory for Andy was perfect; the weather even cooperated. It was magical. I think I am in love.

Now for the bad news. Thanksgiving without Emily was horrible. We went to my grandma's house for dinner. Everywhere I looked, I kept picturing myself with Emily last year, playing with her, and keeping her out of trouble. Except I wasn't really remembering her alive and there, but I was remembering the photographs my mom and I took that day. More and more, I find it harder and harder to picture Emily alive in my mind. When I try to imagine the details of her face, it is just photographs I've seen. The only thing I am able to remember that is not a photograph is still the image of her lying in her casket. After a while I gave up trying; I skipped dinner and spent the day on the bed in my grandparents' spare bedroom.

My other bad news is Andy broke up with me two days ago. It was Saturday night; my mom and Aunt Shari went out to a movie. I babysat Forti and Prio. My mom said Andy could come over, rent movies, and order pizza. Everything was going fine. We watched *Home Alone* with Forti and Prio. We sat shoulder to shoulder on the couch and for a while I rested my head on his shoulder. I tucked Forti and Prio into bed;

when I came back downstairs, Andy looked really sad.

"Are you ready to watch our movie?" I asked.

"I am going back to California in less than two weeks."

"I know."

"I don't want to go." I sat down in the small space between Andy and the arm of the couch; he moved away. "I think we should just be friends."

I stared at my hands clenched together in my lap.

He said, "If we are just friends, I think it won't hurt so much when I have to leave."

I looked up; his face was blurry through my tears. "Don't you think it is a little late for that?" He shrugged his shoulders. "Why are you doing this?"

"We can still spend the day together next Sunday when you get home from your dad's like we planned."

I screamed at him, "Get out of here!" I slammed the door behind his back. Why did he have to ruin his last few days here? I was awake most of the night crying; the last time I looked at my clock it was 4:48 a.m.

You will never guess what happened next. My mom knocked on my door at 10 a.m. and said Andy was on the phone for me. He acted like nothing had happened; he acted like we were actually friends. He came over in the afternoon to study for our biology test. I made us hot cocoa and everything was the same as it had been, except we didn't hold hands and he didn't kiss me goodbye. It made me mad.

On Monday, he walked me home after school like always but he didn't hold my hand like always. As we got closer to my house, I clenched my fists tighter at my sides. I felt like I was a pot of water on the stove getting ready to boil. He kept talking about the science test, going over every question, trying to figure out if he answered them correctly. When we got to the front of my house, I crossed my arms in front of me and stared at him.

"I'd better get going," he said, and then turned to walk away.

"Fine. See you later, *friend*."

He turned around. "Is something wrong?"

Then my anger changed to fear and I realized if I made Andy mad, he might not want to be my friend either. So I just smiled and said, "No. I was just saying see you later." He waved and left.

I don't want to screw up the little time I have left with Andy here by fighting with him, but I just don't see how simply not kissing or holding hands is going to make it any easier when he goes back to California. Do you? Maybe I am missing something. Please tell me what you think.

Please don't be surprised if my next letter is very depressing;

by the time you get this and write me back, Andy will be gone and I will be enduring the holidays without Emily. Which reminds me, do you celebrate Christmas or New Year's? We usually have a Christmas Eve party at my grandma's house with my great aunts and uncles, my grandparents' neighbors, and friends. On Christmas Day, we go back for a big ham dinner. Then, we do it all over again on New Year's Eve and New Year's Day. Since my dad left, I have to miss one or the other, though, because I have to go stay with him. This year, we are there for Christmas Eve and Christmas Day, and I think we are going to Nikki's parents' house for Christmas Eve. She is cooking turkey dinner for us and my dad on Christmas Day, which I'm sure will be delicious (not!). But at least it will be different and maybe it will keep my mind off Emily and Andy.

I hope the war continues to stay away from Rijeka! Write me back when you can.

Your friend,
Ami

*   *   *   *   *

16 December 1991

Dear Ami,

Andy sounds like a really mixed-up boy. I'm sorry he broke up with you. By now you should have had your last weekend "date" together. I hope he realized how stupid he was acting. I agree with you. By now, "just being friends" is not going to change your feelings. If he wanted to avoid missing you when he goes back to California, he should have never spent any time with you in first place. Now it is too late. He should just enjoy the time he has left. He will be going back home whether he spends the time being miserable without a girlfriend or having fun with his girlfriend. Did he say he will write to you or call you on the telephone after he goes back?

Marija's belly is getting huge! Sometimes it even has corners. Marija says that is the baby's elbows or knees. How odd that must feel! I hope your upcoming holidays are better than your "Thanksgiving." We don't have a Thanksgiving in Croatia but we learned about this American holiday in school. We also learned about your Christmas holidays. Ours are a little different. Instead of on 24 December, St. Nicholas visited kids here on 5 December. We leave our boots or socks on window and then, if we've been good, when we wake up on 6 December, they are filled with candies and chocolate. The Roman Catholics or Croats celebrate Christmas much like Americans. On 24, they don't eat meat, drink milk, or consume anything that comes from animals, just fish and dried figs. They have mass at church at the end of night for an hour. The next day, they have a huge dinner with roast pig and Sarma which is ground beef, rice, and other things rolled in cabbage. They also have mashed potatoes, prosciutto, cheeses, pickles, cookies, and cakes. The Catholic Orthodox's or Serb Christmas is celebrated on 6 and 7 January. Some people go out to party on 6 January. At 4 a.m. on 7 January, we have to go to church for the Uranak service. Later in the day, we have our meal with basically same things the Roman Catholics have on 25 December. For Roman Catholics, 6 January is Three Kings Day and is the day they take down their Christmas trees and decorations. With the war, this year we won't even be able to go to church for Christmas. All of the Catholic Orthodox churches are closed.

The war is still at its worst in Dubrovnik but the rest of Croatia has not been spared. Dubrovnik is still being bombed and the people there are without water, electricity, or telephones. We have heard on television Serbs are blamed for the war. Maybe that is why the tragedy of the war has struck someone else in my family. The wife of my mom's uncle killed herself. My mom's uncle is a civil engineer and his wife was a chemical engineer. They lived in Zagreb and had three kids. Because they got so many threats they would be killed, she made a poison concoction and killed herself. I didn't know them that well but it is still so sad. We have also heard Croatia is getting closer to being recognized as its own country. I know my parents wanted Croatia to stay part of Yugoslavia but maybe if it stays its own country now, the fighting will stop and we can get back to normal. And maybe go visit my grandparents. I miss them so much!

Write back soon!

Your friend,
Nada

Jodie Toohey

CHAPTER NINETEEN

Like he said he would, Andy showed up at my house a half hour after I got home from Dad and Nikki's at ten o'clock on Sunday morning. Aunt Shari drove us to the mall. We sat on a bench watching the fountain and beyond it, the kids waiting in line to sit on Santa's lap. We were quiet but I didn't need words. I just wanted to savor the moments before Andy went back home. He bought me a hamburger in the food court and we went to see a movie, thankfully a comedy. We never held hands but sat with our arms touching. After that, we walked through the mall and discussed the funniest parts of the movie. Aunt Shari picked us up at three and we spent the remaining two plus hours of our day together studying for our semester finals.

At school the next day and for the rest of the week, I didn't see Andy much. He seemed to avoid me. When I tried to talk to him at his locker, he was quiet. Krissa had invited us over to her house after our last day of school before winter break on December 19th. I hadn't seen him all that day and finally caught up to him at his locker at the end of the lunch period.

"Do you want to walk to Krissa's for her cookie decorating party?" I asked.

"I don't think I'm going." He pulled his books from his top locker shelf. "I need to start packing."

"It will only be a couple of hours. I can help you pack if you want me to."

Andy held the edge of the metal locker door. "When I think of going to the party, I think of you, which reminds me I have to leave soon, which makes me sad." He slammed the metal shut with his flat hand and walked away. I watched his back until it turned through the doors to the cafeteria and went to my own fifth period class.

After school, the halls were empty. I took extra time to fill my backpack with everything from my locker I thought I might need during winter break: a notebook, a pen, and a couple of library books. Andy came up and leaned against my neighbor's locker.

"Hi," he said.

"Hi." I zipped my backpack. "Did you change your mind about going to Krissa's?"

"No. I just wanted to say…" Andy hesitated and I waited. His voice cracked, "I just wanted to say have fun." He walked past me down the hall.

"Andy!" He stopped and rested his books on the edge of a trash can, but he didn't turn toward me. I left my backpack laying next to my open locker, walked in front of him, and turned to face him. He stared at the floor. I wrapped my arms behind his neck; he hugged me back. He breathed in hard and then squeezed tighter. "I know," I whispered. I thought I knew.

When we let go, I looked past Andy. I shut my locker

door, picked up my backpack, and walked away without looking back.

The next day, Andy's aunt and uncle were leaving with him to take him to the airport at one o'clock in the afternoon; I went over to say goodbye at noon. When I got to their house, Andy was shooting basketballs into the hoop alongside the driveway. When he saw me, he caught the ball and held it against his side.

"Is it noon already?" he said, letting the ball fall. It bounced decreasingly away until it rolled into the grass.

I walked toward him and stopped, facing him a few feet away. "Are you all ready to go?" I asked.

"I've got everything packed up and in the trunk of the car."

We chatted about the last days of school, the semester finals, and the school's attempt at Christmas dinner. I finally worked up the courage to ask for his address in California.

"I have something for you." He disappeared into the side door of his aunt and uncle's powder-blue ranch house. He returned with an envelope and I opened it. "It's my address and my picture."

I unfolded the piece of notebook paper; an address in California was written in neat capital letters and it encapsulated a wallet size school photo. I remembered the day it was taken. He wore a button up shirt with criss-crossing blue and green lines. He smiled at me from the photograph as he'd done so many times over the previous months.

"Thanks." I folded the paper and returned it to the envelope.

"Will you write me?" Andy asked.

"Sure," I said. "Maybe I will write you today so you will

get it fast. Then you can write me back."

"Sounds good." He pushed his hands into his coat pockets, tilted his head, and half-smiled.

I swallowed. "I'd better get going. I told my mom I would be back soon."

"Okay."

Andy reached out and pulled me toward him. We pulled apart and he walked toward the basketball lying in the frozen grass. He picked it up and held it against his chest.

"Thank you," he said.

"Bye," I said. I heard the basketball on the pavement as I crossed the street. Before I turned the corner out of sight, I turned back. Andy looked at me holding the basketball to his chest like he was preparing to pass it. His face was crumpled. I smiled as bright as I could and waved. If I'd known, I would have run back to him and hugged him tight longer.

CHAPTER TWENTY

Even though I knew the holidays would be hell without Emily, I was a little grateful for the distraction away from waiting for Andy's letter. When I woke up on Christmas Eve morning, I packed my overnight bag and helped Forti pack hers. I walked down the stairs and put them next to the front door. Dad and Nikki were due to arrive any minute, but it was unusually quiet. By then Prio was normally engaged in idle banter with whoever would listen, especially on Christmas Eve when Santa was expected to visit. All I heard was muffled cartoons upstairs. I went into the kitchen. My mom and Aunt Shari were sitting at the table, their four eyes typically red, a box of facial tissues between them with one waving from the top of the box waiting for release.

My mom jumped up when she saw me. She looked at the digital clock on the back of the stove. "It's almost ten. Your dad will be here any minute." She yelled toward the front of the house, "Forti! Prio! Ami, will you go check on them? I sent Prio up an hour ago to get dressed and I sent Forti up a half an hour ago to hurry him along."

I opened Prio's door to find them both on the bed laughing at a cartoon. Prio wore blue jeans, a pajama shirt with a spaceship painted on the front, and one white sock.

"What are you two doing? Dad's on his way." They looked at each other and then blankly at me. I shut off the TV. "Where is your shirt?" Prio pointed to his closet. "Stand up." I pulled Prio's pajama shirt over his head, stripped a shirt off a hanger in his closet, and slipped it on to his scrawny body. "Get your sock. Come on!" I walked out, but noticed when I got halfway down the stairs, they weren't behind me. "Forti! Prio!" When I was a few more stairs down, the doorbell rang. "Hurry!" I yelled up.

My dad drove us directly to Nikki's parents' house. They lived a half an hour away. I sat in the front seat, stared out the window, and pretended to sleep whenever I thought my dad was looking my way or was getting ready to try to talk to me. Forti and Prio chattered in the back seat with each other about presents and Christmas cookies. Nikki's parents lived in a two-story brick house, symmetrical with four windows downstairs and four windows upstairs, all lit with fake stick candles. The house smelled sweet, hot, and like partially burnt microwave popcorn. An older version of Nikki with the same perfectly placed just-out-of-place hair, but in grey, met us at the door.

"Hello, Don, I'm so glad you could make it. Can I take your coats?" Forti and Prio dropped their coats at her feet. My dad slowly unzipped his to reveal a bright red sweater adorned with a satin appliquéd light- up Christmas tree.

"Oh, good, you wore the sweater." Nikki's mom took my dad's coat; when she turned her back to him, he looked at me and shrugged his shoulders. I halfway smiled at him. I would have laughed if I wasn't trying so hard not to barf from the burnt popcorn smell.

"Would you like to string popcorn for the tree?" Nikki's mom asked, but before she could finish her sentence, Forti and Prio were picking burnt popcorn out of the bowl. Forti made a face and started to spit on Nikki's relatives' shoes and my dad rushed over.

"Would you like me to take your coat, Ami?" Nikki's mother asked.

"No, thank you," I said. "I'm not feeling very good. I think I'm going to sit outside on the step for a minute."

"Sure. Or you might be more comfortable on the patio."

"Okay," I said. Nikki's mom gently guided me through the house with her hand against the small of my back. She led me to a chair with a big green checked cushion sitting on the edge of a brick patio facing a thick bunch of trees toward the far corner of the yard.

Nikki's mom pointed to the chair. "I like to sit out here. Sometimes you can see deer back there."

"Thank you." I sat down.

"You can sit out here for as long as you want to. If you get cold, hungry, or thirsty, just come on back in."

I promised I would. When I heard the click of the vinyl French doors closing, I leaned into the chair and looked up at the grey sky. I wondered if Emily was up there somewhere looking down at me, and whether Andy was also looking up at a grey sky, or if he was looking up at the sunny ones for which California is famous. I looked toward the house and saw my father at the door, but as he reached for the handle, Nikki's mom grabbed his sleeve and led him away. She patted his shoulder with her free hand and I thought that I kind of liked Nikki's mom. Other than their appearances, they weren't a lot alike.

I spent most of the day sitting outside. I was starting to get cold when Dad brought me a thick blanket and a cup of hot cocoa. "Mrs. Carcassy thought you might like these."

I tucked the blanket around my legs and my body up to just beneath my armpits and took the steaming mug. "Thank you," I said and then looked straight ahead, sipping. My dad stood next to me for a few minutes. He lightly squeezed my right shoulder before returning to the house. I only came in to eat a little ham for dinner and open gifts. Prio, Forti, and I all got bright red sweaters to match my dad's.

I found out Nikki's mom knitted them herself. Normally, I might've refused, but Nikki's mom had been so nice and I suspected she was the driving force behind everyone thankfully leaving me alone, that when she asked, I slipped the sweater on over my shirt, smoothed my static flyaway hair, and smiled for her photograph.

That night, my dad let Forti and Prio sleep on the couch in the living room next to the Christmas tree so they could try to catch Santa filling their stockings nailed to the wall near the top of the paper fireplace they'd colored earlier at Nikki's parents. That meant I got the guest room all to myself and could let flow the emotions I'd had to stifle the last several weeks of sharing a room with Forti. I tried to ignore it at first. I lay in bed staring up at the ceiling. I started thinking about last Christmas Eve with Emily. She was a little bit over fourteen months old and I could do more with her than hold her and open her presents for her. I remembered how I lifted a corner of the wrapping paper. She would put her face right up to the paper to try to see what was inside. She'd stick her fingers in and pull the paper away a little further. When she saw the bright logo of the toy's maker, she squealed and then ripped the remaining wrap off in a matter of seconds. I gave

Emily three gifts last year for Christmas, more than I got my own brother and sister, but seeing her repeat the peek, squeal, and rip process made it worth it. One of the gifts was a teddy bear I sewed in home economics class that fall. When I gave it to her, she hugged it tight under her chin and I had to hide it to get her to open the rest of her gifts.

I had the teddy bear sitting on a shelf in my room with a picture of Emily and me propped up on its legs. I thought about the day I'd spent alone talking to no one and a stabbing hole began to grow in my chest. At first the tears slipped quietly out of the corners of my eyes. I tried to think of something different; something happier. I thought about Andy but that just made my quiet tears turn to sobs I had to muffle with my pillow.

Jodie Toohey

CHAPTER TWENTY-ONE

December 30, 1991

Dear Nada,

Happy Holidays! I survived my Christmas and I hope you have a good Christmas next week. I spent most of Christmas Eve sitting on the patio at Nikki's parents' house. On Christmas Day, Nikki attempted to cook dinner for my dad, Forti, Prio, and me. We had pre-cooked turkey from the freezer. Nikki cooked it under the broiler in the oven, so the outside was crunchy and the middle was cold. She served it with lumpy mashed potatoes and watery, near-flavorless gravy. My dad took the first bite and said it was delicious. Then Forti, Prio, and I tried a bite at the same time. As soon as Prio swallowed, tears started falling from his eyes. He screamed at my dad, "You liar! This is yucky!"

Puffs of air escaped Forti's lips as she started to cry. "What's wrong?" asked my dad.

Forti pushed her plate toward the middle of the table. "I want Mommy."

It broke my heart to see my brother and sister so upset. I got up, walked around the table, and pulled them both toward me to hug them. Then I started to cry for reasons other than the disastrous dinner.

Nikki yelled, "I'm sorry I ruined your Christmas!" as she knocked over her dining room chair in the process of running to their bedroom and slamming the door. My dad silently cut the crunchy away from the cold parts of the turkey, took a loaf of bread from the cupboard, and made four sandwiches. We cried as we ate them with plain potato chips. That was my Christmas dinner. Nikki and Dad comforted my siblings' hurt by not speaking to them until they took us home that evening. They just mumbled, "Goodbye," and walked out the door.

Andy has been gone for ten days and I still have not heard anything from him. He should have received my letter and Christmas card, but I haven't received anything in return. I miss him so much. Maybe he has been too busy visiting with his family and celebrating Christmas to have time to write me back.

Tomorrow is New Year's Eve. I'm babysitting Forti and Prio while my mom and Aunt Shari go out. I wonder if I will ever stop thinking about what would be different on certain days if Emily was still here, because as soon as I wrote down I would be babysitting my brother and sister, I wanted to write I should be babysitting Emily while my Aunt Shari and Uncle Matt go out. But I didn't because I think I have written that so many times you are probably getting tired of it. Anyway, I hope you have a good Christmas holiday January 6th and 7th!

Your friend,
Ami

*   *   *   *   *

I lay on my bed, my right ear attached to my stereo with a headphone earpiece blasting NKOTB to avoid waking up Forti who was napping in anticipation of staying up long enough to ring in 1992. My left ear listened for the mail truck. If there was no letter from Andy, it would be two days before I would even possibly hear from him. By then, he would be back home for almost two weeks.

I heard the squeak of the mail truck's brakes stopping at our neighbor's mailbox. I yanked the cord of my headphones and could still faintly hear the music, so I pushed the pause button on my tape player. I closed my bedroom door behind me as quietly as I could and hopped down the stairs. I watched the mail carrier put letters into my next-door neighbor's box. He drove toward our mailbox. *Stop, stop, stop,* I pleaded in my head. He slowed to a stop, reached his arm out of the window, and pulled open the mailbox door. He shoved several white envelopes in; I waited until he was a few houses down the road before I went out. I put on my shoes but didn't tie them or take a coat. I flipped through the letters in front of the mailbox while standing on the side of the road in the snow; bills, greeting card envelopes addressed generically to "The Sinkeys," and our weekly fat envelope of coupons, but nothing for me specifically and nothing from California. Numbness swept over me and I shivered, suddenly cold.

I dropped the mail on the kitchen counter and went to my room. I was face down on my bed with my pillow over my head before I remembered Forti had been sleeping. I stretched my neck back over my shoulder. Her bed was empty. I folded the pillow around my head and cried. *Did something bad happen to him? Did he forget about me? Has he been too busy? Did it hurt him too much to think about writing me? Did he ever care about me at all?*

I cried until I must have fallen asleep because the next thing I remembered was opening my eyes to see my mom's face peering under the pillow.

"Taking a nap?" she asked.

"I guess so." I pushed the pillow off my head and sat up, hoping the redness of my crying eyes had faded.

"Good idea. Forti and Prio are adamant they're staying up until midnight." My eyes had not yet adjusted from being buried under my pillow, so I could barely see her through my squinted eyes. "Come downstairs; we're getting ready to leave."

I squinted at my clock: 4:15. "Already?" I asked.

"Grandma is making us come over for chili before we go out." She turned toward me from the doorway to my room. "Real good plan, isn't it?"

"Sure." I sighed and pulled myself up from my bed.

"Are you coming?" my mom yelled up the stairs. "I want to show you how to cook the pizza snacks before we go."

I leaned my head out into the hallway, bracing myself on the edge of the door and the door casing. "I've made those a dozen times." I hollered down the stairs loud enough so I hoped my mom could hear. She popped her head back, pivoting on the ball on top of the last railing post at the bottom of the stairs.

"Fine," she said. She threw her hands up in the air. "You've got fifteen minutes."

I pushed the door closed hard but not quite a slam. I plopped into my desk chair and hit the top with both elbows. A pen bounced to the floor. I held my hot cheeks in my hands for a few seconds before pushing my face through them toward the desktop. I grabbed the hair behind my ears with each clenched fist and silently screamed, pushing air up in my throat and straining it against my eyes until I could see tiny sparks of light.

Jodie Toohey

CHAPTER TWENTY-TWO

18 January 1992

Dear Ami,

I'm sorry your Christmas was so terrible. My holiday was quite good. Guess what? I finally got to visit my grandparents in Bosnia. We could not take our usual four-hour route because of the fighting still happening in the Krajina so we had to go to Ljubljana to take a bus through Slovenia around through Hungary through Serbia to Bosnia. It took us 24 hours to get there! But it was worth it to be at my grandparents' for holiday. Tata got home on Friday, 3 January and we left while it was still dark out on 4 January but we arrived at my grandparents' on 5 January, in time for the celebrations and feast. Stevo and Marija stayed home to watch our house because their baby is due so soon.

It appears as if my old country of Yugoslavia is gone forever and I now almost officially live in the country of

Croatia. A day or two before the Roman Catholic Christmas, the news said Germany views Croatia and Slovenia as independent countries. The rest of Europe did same just within the last couple of days. I am hopeful this new year of 1992 will be better for my country. Once again I am thankful to be living in Rijeka, relatively far away from the worst fighting. We have heard that in towns near front lines like Sisak, Karlovac, Zadar, Gospić, Osijek, Vinkovci, and Zagreb, Serbs who did not leave had bombs put in their houses and in their cars. If I would have heard that when most of fighting was happening, I would have not only been afraid to go to sleep at night but I would have never left my house for fear I would be blown up when I got into our car to leave or when we came back home. I hope I will not have to worry about that anymore. During first few days of this year, the fighters signed a peace-keeping plan and cease-fire in Sarajevo in Bosnia. This is why my parents decided finally it would be okay to go to visit my grandparents. Tata will still be working in Italy, but hopefully, he will be able to come home more often.

My aunts and uncles who live by my grandparents' came over on 6 January. They drank Rakija. It is a moonshine made from plums. They also played cards. Maja and I bundled up in our coats, took the cows to meadow to graze, and fed the chickens. We helped my grandma make doughnuts. They were delicious!

Have you received a letter from Andy yet? I'm sure he has not forgotten about you and still cares about you. He is probably just busy seeing all of his friends and family he couldn't see while he was away from home. I hope you hear from him soon! Maybe he will call you on the telephone instead. I think that would be better than a letter. Write me back when you can.

Your "Croatian" friend,
Nada

*   *   *   *   *

Nada wrote that letter a week ago today, I thought, sitting cross-legged at the end of the pier. The river was covered in ice but for a few open pools; once in a while a piece would break loose and float away, but it couldn't get very far before it was stopped with a crack by solid ice on the down- current side of the pool. I was happy for Nada; glad the war seemed to be over in her country and that she got to visit her family. I felt jealous for a moment. I thought it was because Nada's life was getting back to normal while I knew mine would never be normal again. Then I remembered her dad was still not going to be living at home most of the time and that she wasn't even living in the same country as she used to be. I realized her life would never be normal again either. But I still felt jealous. I realized I felt jealous because Nada seemed to be happy or at least okay with her new "normal" while I still felt like I was drowning in dark storm clouds.

Jodie Toohey

CHAPTER TWENTY-THREE

I didn't answer Nada's January 18th letter. I didn't want to dampen her adjustment to her new life with news of the same old turmoil of mine. I sent Andy another letter right after I got Nada's. I hoped he would write me back so I would have at least a morsel of good news to share with Nada in my next letter. After school, I stopped at the mailbox like I did every day, trying to suppress any hope in what I already knew was a futile attempt to decrease the impending disappointment. I flipped through the mail and saw my own name and address in the upper left hand corner of one of the envelopes. I dropped the rest of the mail in the snow and read the yellow sticker on the last letter I sent to Andy. *Undeliverable. Unable to Forward.* I stared at the dotted type and reread it as it blurred from my tears.

I picked up the mail from the snow, pushed it back into the mailbox, and slammed the door shut. I folded my returned letter and shoved it in my coat pocket. I barely opened my front door wide enough to toss my backpack inside by the front door. "Mom, I'm going for a walk," I yelled into the house. I heard the first syllable from her mouth and closed the door.

I ran as fast as I could toward the river, pounding my feet into the asphalt until my legs ached and my chest began to burn. I choked and slowed to a walk. I sat down on the pier and read the words I had written to Andy. Now he would never know what I had to say. He would never know I had set him free; that I had told him I would always care about him and would be waiting when he wanted to contact me. Now it didn't matter. I tore the letter up into confetti pieces and let them fall from my hand toward the icy water.

I lay down on the concrete pier and pulled my knees into my chest. I sobbed. The world was silent. Nobody noticed. I took my mind back until the first time I met Andy. I replayed everything I ever said to him, everything I ever did, everything he ever said to me, and I tried to figure out why. *The Andy I knew wouldn't have moved without telling me. It had to be something I did, but what? What changed between the day we said goodbye and now? Did something bad happen to him? Why does everyone I care about leave me?*

My screams echoed in the hollow winter air. My knuckles whitened and my fingers stiffened in the cold. I finally ran out of tears and sat up. The river seemed to whisper to me, "Jump in or don't. Time to decide." I realized I was tired of crying myself to sleep at night; tired of feeling hopeless and I just wanted it to stop. I was tired of the beast inside my head berating me, telling me there was no reason to live, and it would never get any better. I wanted to die but I was afraid. I hoped there was a heaven and I hoped Emily was there watching over me, but I wasn't sure. I had always questioned blind faith and sought proof. As terrible as it was, I knew what life was and that comforted me. I knew what it felt like to drag myself out of bed in the morning, at first hopeful, and then remembering what was gone. But with death I didn't know if my pain would end or if I would simply just end with no chance to play with Prio and Forti or do any of the other things that used to make me smile. But I knew the pain would be over. My feet dangled over the iced muddy Mississippi and my hands clamped over the edge of the cement pier.

A click behind me made me jump. I looked back over my shoulder and saw Larry Benson lean his bike on its kickstand. He walked toward me. I thought that he looked different and then realized he was wearing glasses. I pulled my feet toward my chest and jumped up without using my hands.

"Hi, Ami," Larry said.

"Hi." I thought about pushing past him and running away. On my many walks through town, I had often hoped to run into Larry, but at the same time, I was afraid I would see him. I didn't know what to feel: anger or excitement? Should I be mean? Should I be nice?

"I'm glad I found you. Your mom said you might be here." Larry slid his bare hand along the pier's railing.

"She did?"

"I went to your house to talk to you. She said you went for a walk."

I walked up the pier toward Larry. Suddenly cold, I pushed my hands as far as I could into my coat pockets.

"She said she thought you like to come here." I looked at the crumbling cement of the pier's floor. "So she was right?"

"Yes. I like it here."

"Anyway, can I talk to you?"

"I guess so," I said. We sat down on one of the benches facing the water. It seemed like I waited for hours before

Larry finally spoke.

"I saw Krissa earlier today."

Here we go. If he wants me to fix him up with her after everything he's done, I thought, *he's crazy.* I turned and glared at him, but he just stared across the river.

"She said you were mad at me. But I had no idea."

He had no idea?

"She told me when you called me that day that you wanted to talk to me about your cousin's death. I don't know why, but girls call me and they don't even want anything. I thought you were just another one of them and I wanted to watch the game." Larry stood up and hung by his waist over the railing. He turned his head and looked at me out of the corner of his eye. "I'm really sorry. I felt so bad when I heard your cousin died. I probably should've known that was why you were calling. But I didn't. Then she said you thought I was ignoring you on the Fourth of July, but I was embarrassed because I couldn't see it was you. I found out later I need to wear glasses."

He stood up and wiped his face with the back of his coat sleeve. I saw it was wet with tears as he dropped his arm back to his side before walking away from me back up the pier toward the shore. "So I'm sorry you thought I was a jerk all of these months. If I'd known that was why you were calling, I would have been nicer."

I swallowed and tried to keep my tears in my eyes. "Okay," was all I could say.

"I have to go. I told my mom I wouldn't be gone this long," he said. He pushed his bike's kickstand up with his foot and threw his leg over its top bar. "Hope you have a good weekend. Maybe we'll talk in class?" he said.

"Sure." I waved weakly as he rode away.

CHAPTER TWENTY-FOUR

I sat back down on the bench and thought about what had just happened. I watched the sun setting beyond the trees across the river, with their shadows creeping toward me over the ice, and thought, *this is it.* I would either see the sun again or I wouldn't. I would either see my mom, brother, and sister again or I wouldn't. I would graduate from high school, go to college, get married, and have kids or I wouldn't. I would either feel my lungs fill with the warm humid summer or the frozen winter air or I wouldn't. I could live or I could die. And it was my choice alone. I realized I had always had complete control of that. I knew if I jumped into the river I would never see the sun, my mom, Forti, Prio, Andy, or Larry Benson again. I knew I would never graduate high school, go to college, get married, have kids, or breathe; that was certain. This certainty comforted me some; knowing was less scary than not knowing. But, for everything I knew would happen should I jump in the river, there was a whole other reality I did not know. I knew if I killed myself, I would never get to do those things and if I didn't, I still might not get to do those things. But with living, there was a chance I would and I realized that chance gave me hope. As long as I had hope, I wanted to live. If I jumped in the river, my story would end, but I wanted to see what would happen with Larry next week.

I decided in that moment that to live was my final decision. I would never again put myself in the position of making the decision between life and death; that no matter what, I would not consider death an option.

I wrote a letter to Nada that night before bed.

* * * * *

February 7, 1992

Dear Nada,

I'm sorry it has been so long since I've written you a letter. I am very glad you had good holidays and that you were able to go visit your grandparents. I am also so glad you are no longer worried about war coming to Rijeka. You inspire me. I have decided if you have been brave enough to live through a real war in your country and still find a reason to smile, then I can find a reason to smile after everything I have been through.

I had a revelation earlier today by the river. Something happened to give me hope everything will be okay. I realized it was time to make a decision; that I alone controlled whether I was going to live or die and it was time to decide one way or another. I, obviously, decided to live. After making that final decision, I stood up from where I was sitting on the pier as the first wave of darkness spread over the water. I knew before long all there would be was black ink between me and the opposite shore. I sucked in a deep breath and turned to walk toward home. When I got to the top of the hill, I started to run.

As I approached the front of my house, I noticed every light inside was turned on and I thought I had not seen it that bright in a long time, if ever. The windows were steamed over and I met the smell of chicken noodle soup when I opened the door.

"Mom, Ami's home," Forti yelled from the couch where he was watching TV.

My mom walked into the living room. "Good, she's just in time for Grandma's famous chicken noodle soup." She flipped the towel she had wiped her hands on over her shoulder. "Everything okay?" she asked. I shook my head yes as I hung my coat's hood on the hook by the front door.

I sat down at the table with my grandma, Aunt Shari, Mom, Forti, and Prio and thought about how Emily was so much a missing piece. Forti and Prio held oyster crackers above their bowls of steaming soup. They counted, "One, two, three," let go of them, and giggled as they splashed in the broth. My grandma and mom laughed as they told them to stop in stereo. Aunt Shari smiled faintly and watched them, undoubtedly thinking about Emily and how she would have been copying her older cousins. Today my world is this; eating soup with these people, all of us knowing someone who should be there is not. We are wounded and broken but still trudging through to find a moment of happiness in the silly carefree acts of a nine year old and a five year old, the only thing on this earth that can truly make our hearts sing.

It is weird, but that simple thing made me feel like maybe everything will be okay for me someday. I will never forget Emily or Andy, but Emily will be watching over me as my guardian angel. And maybe someday Andy will tell me why he didn't write and his letter came back; until I have a way to find *him*, all I can do is wait patiently.

I hope that Stevo and Marija's baby is happy and healthy and that you get to spend lots of time holding him or her. I hope also that he or she gets to live a long, long life so you will know the joy that watching a baby grow can bring. And I hope he or she will love you as much as I know Emily loved me.

Always your American pen pal friend,
Ami

*   *   *   *   *

I enclosed the letter in an envelope and got it ready to mail. After pulling on extra pants and a sweatshirt under my winter coat, I went out to play with Forti and Prio in the night's fresh snow.

AUTHOR'S NOTE

Croatia is a country located in eastern Europe along the eastern shore of the Adriatic Sea across from the northern boot portion of Italy. Until the early 1990s, Croatia was a Republic within the former country of Yugoslavia, which also included the now independent countries of Slovenia, Bosnia-Herzegovina, Serbia, Montenegro, and Macedonia. From the end of World War II until 1980, Yugoslavia was a communist country held together under the leadership of Tito. From Tito's death until Croatia and Slovenia declared independence, Presidents from each of the Republics rotated leadership of Yugoslavia.

The vast majority of Croatia's population follows the Roman Catholic religion and approximately twelve percent follow the Catholic Orthodox religion. The term "Croat" is synonymous with Roman Catholic followers while "Serb" is synonymous with Catholic Orthodox followers. Unlike in the United States, religious views are central to the area's government and politics.

On June 25, 1991, the majority of people living in the

Republic of Croatia voted to split away from Yugoslavia to become its own independent country. After the declaration, war broke out between the Croats, who wanted to separate, and the Serbs, who wanted to keep Yugoslavia united. On December 23, 1991, Germany recognized Croatia as an independent country with the rest of Europe following by mid-January, 1992. The United States, as well as Russia and China, did not recognize Croatia as its own country until early April, 1992.

Though the accounts in this book are fictional, personal accounts and research shows Serbs living in Croat-majority areas were discriminated against. Their neighbors and friends suddenly shunned them, they received threat letters and calls, and they were discriminated against in school, where their religion was listed in their student records. Many have written about how Serbs and Croats committed acts of ethnic cleansing against each other and many people were driven from their homes. Children often carried out their daily lives, essentially as usual, but lay awake at night fearing someone may break into kill them or drive their families to a "home" where they may have never visited.

I was seventeen to eighteen years old during this period and, being a teenager, I was engrossed in my own life and don't recall knowing a great deal about the war in Yugoslavia. What I do recall hearing was about the acts of "Serbian insurgents," and in my research for writing this book, I learned Serbs were largely blamed by American media for the war. However, the war occurred *between* the Serbs and the Croats who were both guilty of killing and committing crimes against the other. Readers are encouraged to consider the world outside of their own lives, towns, and country and be skeptical of media accounts of events they have not personally witnessed.

Jodie Toohey

SELECTED BIBLIOGRAPHY

Carroll, Chris. "Serbs Face the Future: One Nation Divisible." *National Geographic*, July 31, 2009. http://ngm.nationalgeographic. com/print/2009/07/serbs/carroll-text.

Cockburn, Alexander. "Beat the Devil: Hating Serbs is Fun." *The Nation*, October 16, 1995, 411-412.

Dragnich, Alex N. *Serbs and Croats: The Struggle in Yugoslavia.* New York: Harcourt Brace Jovanovich, 1992.

Eyewitness Travel: Croatia. New York: DK Publishing, Inc., 2007.

Freedom from Despair: A Young Man's Journey from Despair, A Nation's Struggle for Freedom. DVD. Written and Directed by Brenda Brkusic. 2004.

Filipovic, Zlata. *Zlata's Diary: A Child's Life in Sarajevo, 2nd ed.* Des Moines, Iowa: Perfection Learning, 2006.

Gagnon, V.P., Jr.. *The Myth of Ethnic War: Serbia and Croatia in the 1990s.* Ithaca and London: Cornell University Press, 2004.

Gazi, Stephen. *A History of Croatia.* New York: Barnes & Noble Books, 1993.

Goldstein, Ivo. *Croatia: A History.* Montreal & Kingston: McGill- Queen's University Press, 1999.

Kaplan, Robert D. *Balkan Ghosts: A Journey Through History.* New York: St. Martin's Press, 2005.

Neier, Aryeh. "Watching Rights." *The Nation*, January 9/16, 1995, 43.

Tanner, Marcus. *Croatia: A Nation Forged in War, 2nd ed.* New Haven: Yale University Press, 2001.

Yugoslavia: The Avoidable War. Directed by George Bogdanich. 1999.

ABOUT THE AUTHOR

Jodie Toohey is the author of two novels – *Missing Emily: Croatian Life Letters* and *Melody Madson – May It Please the Court?* – as well as two poetry collections – *Crush and Other Love Poems for Girls* and *The Other Side of Crazy*. Her next novel, *Taming the Twisted*, will be released in August, 2015.

When Jodie is not writing poetry or fiction, she is helping authors, soon-to-be-authors, and want-to-be authors from pre-idea to reader through her company, Wordsy Woman Author Services. She lives in Iowa with her husband, daughter, son, and beagle, Maizey.

Learn more about Jodie's books and sign up to receive updates at jodietoohey.com.
Learn more about her authors services at wordsywomanforauthors.com.

www.ingramcontent.com/pod-product-compliance
Lightning Source LLC
Chambersburg PA
CBHW050943120626
46552CB00001B/353